Crashing Into Love

By

Gregory Jonathan Scott

ISBN: 0991467450
ISBN-13: 978-0-9914674-5-7

DEDICATION

To Scott Burkett, my longtime love, companion and greatest friend. You've always stuck by my side, grabbed my hand when I was about to fall, and picked me up when I did.
Thank you for being my Pilot.

To my friend overseas, Tracy Shayler, who has been an inspiration to me from the publication of my first book until now. Thank you, Tracy, for always being there.

Trademark Acknowledgements:

The author acknowledges the trademarked status and trademark owners of the following trademarks mentioned in this work of fiction:

Trademark Acknowledgements: The author acknowledges the trademarked status and trademark owners of the following trademarks mentioned in this work of fiction: Cessna Aircraft Company, Yogi bear Hanna/Barbera, Andrew Christian, Disneyland.

ACKNOWLEDGMENTS

To Tina Marie Adamski, I am thankful again for your dedicated guidance, input, and your patience. With your support, this story got off the ground.

Gregory Jonathan Scott

Chapter 1

Hustling across the private tarmac toward the plane that was waiting there for his arrival, Sean towed his luggage-on-wheels behind him while his overnight bag flopped over his shoulder against his back.

"What the hell?" Fell out of Sean's mouth as he approached the small single-engine aircraft that was supposed to take him from the island of Kauai to Maui. From there, he'd hop on a seven-forty-seven that would take his ass home to the States. His trip to the Hawaiian Islands was over. What he had hoped would be a tropical vacation turned out to be more business than planned. There was no fun on white sand beaches or surfing in the sun.

The plane he was heading toward appeared to be leaning to one side and his first thought was that the piece of crap wasn't taking him anywhere. In fact, it looked like it should be in the nearest aerospace graveyard with the rest of the junk. He wasn't sure about that beast, but felt certain it wasn't flightworthy to take him where he needed to go. What the hell happened to the Cessna business jet he flew to the island in? If he actually made it back to the office on Monday, he would surely bitch slap the goon who booked this rusted puddle jumper. What the hell were they thinking?

He held his boarding pass out, if the flimsy paper could be called that, and checked the airline tag on the tail against the name on the ticket he was holding to see if it matched. It did — shit. That plane was waiting for him. He hoped that because turbo was printed on the engine compartment, it was a good sign. Get in… get up… get down… get out. Boom, boom, boom.

He dragged a deep breath into his lungs and went with it, even though he honestly wanted to turn right around and say to hell with that plane. It didn't look as though it was going to take him anywhere but off the end of the runway and into a ditch.

On Sean's approach, a young man in blue jeans and the typical floral shirt stood at the doorway near the front tire, looking like he was waiting for him, and only him. The man had one foot propped on the wheel-shaft's tie rod, scraping what appeared to be dog shit off the sole of his shoe. How rude for a passenger to use the aircraft for a boot scraper, but people will be people. "Oh, Gawd, it just got better," Sean said.

When Sean reached the poop-shoed man, he

noticed that KALE was scribed on the badge affixed to the pretty shirt he was wearing and below the name was inscribed his title as the captain of the shitty little airplane. That was a surprise, a little unconventional for a pilot's uniform, but it was Hawaii, things were more relaxed than the States, and especially more than his hometown of Los Angeles.

The pilot's handsome face and broad shoulders made up for the way he was dressed, causing Sean to focus on something other than his attire. It didn't take long for Sean to get used to the man's smile either, he jumped right into that. His teeth appeared bright white behind his dark lips and tanned skin, and the way his dark chocolate hair was tossed by the wind in front of his auburn eyes had Sean believing he could be a likable guy. The pilot had to be Hawaiian; the full package Sean was looking at cleared that right up.

"Hello, I'm Sean." Sean pulled his luggage-on-wheels behind him, tugged the satchel higher on his shoulder and stopped in front of Kale without reaching to shake hands. He was expecting a fresh Lei of some kind, but didn't get one. What's up with that?

"Good afternoon sir, I'm Kale," the man said. "Welcome to my plane." He swept one hand toward the plane, showing off the glorious bird that probably needed a push to get it going.

Sean unmistakably grimaced. Was it the bright sunshine piercing his eyes or the fear of the rusty plane and its young pilot in front of him? "Am I the only passenger?" He looked around, hoping for more, thinking safety came in numbers.

"You're it," said Kale. "This four-seater can only hold so much." He grinned. "You can co-pilot, have the window seat next to me."

Sean rolled his eyes and hummed, "Okay then."

"Follow me. You can put your luggage back here, out of the way." Kale took a step, opened up the door beneath the wing and folded the seat forward.

Warily, Sean handed the pilot his wheeled luggage, stepped back out of the way and glanced lustfully at the man's firm, high ass that looked to be awesomely tight. Sean's type of butt for sure and he wouldn't think twice about putting his hands on it.

Backing out of the door, ass first, Kale reached for the other bag over Sean's shoulder.

"Can you keep this one close by? There's a chance I may need it during our flight," Sean said.

With a wry grin, Kale said, "You're allowed one carry on, sir, so taking your bag aboard is fine. We can easily place it in one of the many overhead compartments you will notice along the fuselage ceiling when you enter the aircraft." Kale wasn't serious, just playing at being the perfect flight attendant any passenger would expect.

"Honestly?" A perplexed expression crossed Sean's face and he actually peered into the cabin to see if there were any overhead compartments along the ceiling.

Kale looked at Sean and laughed. "I'm having you on, I was joking. You can place it in the back behind the passenger seat."

Sean grinned back. "Good to know you have

a humorous side. I'm gonna need it on this bloody flight."

"Hey there, you don't like my plane?" Kale asked.

"To be honest, I was expecting a jet," Sean said. "But as long as it gets me from point A to B, I'll be fine with it. Can you make that happen? Get me there in one piece?"

"All righty then, I'm ready if you are." Kale gave Sean the pirate's eye squint for dissing his baby.

"Sure." Sean handed Kale the satchel from his shoulder and backed away. "Do I climb in this side or do I go around?" He pointed. "How the hell does this work?"

"You first have to walk the jet way and when you get to the end of it, you'll find your door of entry. It's on the other side." Kale led Sean around the back of the plane with one hand on his shoulder, impressed by the hardened muscle. "Well now, you're a strong one."

"Are you always this cynical, or do I bring that out in you?" Sean commented.

Chapter 2

"Strap yourself in, mate. As soon as all the lights turn green over here, and we get tower clearance over there, we hit the friendly skies," Kale said with humor. "You need help with that?" He leaned into Sean and clipped his harness into place.

"Why do I have a steering wheel?" Sean asked.

Kale laughed. "It's a control throttle, but you can call it a steering wheel. And that's in case I become incapacitated, so you can fly the plane."

"What the hell?" Sean screeched, "I'm getting out."

"No refunds." Kale pulled on Sean's arm. "Stay, it'll be fun. Look, you have a front row seat to the world and I'm right here to keep you company all the way." He reached in front of Sean and tugged at his safety belts, making sure all were secure. After that, he explained the emergency routine, where the life jackets were located, and what to do if the oxygen masks dropped from the ceiling. The normal shit Sean was used to hearing attendants mention on every flight.

"Got it." Sean gripped the shoulder harness in both hands.

Kale punched buttons, his tone turning more serious when he spoke to the men at the tower. "Ready for takeoff," he said, winking at Sean and giving him a thumbs up.

Sean whimpered, "Oh, Gawd." His legs straining when he pushed them so hard against the floor in front of him.

Slowly the plane taxied to the runway, engine revving, and the spinning propeller at the nose of the plane increasing in speed until it appeared transparent.

Sean looked over at Kale and swallowed, then said, "It's a short trip, everything will be fine. Ju-u-ust fine."

Kale glanced over at Sean and smiled, laid a hand on Sean's knee and squeezed. "Would it make you feel any better if I sang you a lullaby? It might help you relax."

"Go ahead. If you want. Sorry... I'm not good with flying. I don't have any control, and I need to be in control," Sean rambled.

Kale sang, 'Hush little baby.' Keeping one hand pinned to Sean's knee, adding a couple pats in tempo with the song he was singing.

The tower announced, "You are clear for takeoff."

Kale put both hands on the control throttle and pushed it. As quickly as he moved it away from his chest the plane chugged forward, faster and faster down the center of the runway.

In less than ten seconds, the wheels left the ground and they were airborne, flying the friendly skies.

Nervously, Sean pressed himself tightly against his seat, looking out the front window at the clouds coming at him.

After a few minutes passed, Kale concluded his conversation with the tower. The flight deck altimeter showed the plane was at nine hundred feet, letting him know it was okay to pop the autopilot lever into position and let the plane take control.

At that moment Sean calmed down somewhat, loosened his grip on the safety belts and relaxed his trembling legs.

"You alright, my friend?" Kale asked, placing his hand back on Sean's knee.

"Yeah, all good." Sean breathed, looked out the window to his right and saw the Earth moving away. Down below he could only see water that just went on forever, no land anywhere. None. The missing dirt made his heart jump. "How much longer?"

"We just left. It's about a forty-five minute flight to Maui. We'll be there before you know it," Kale mentioned.

"How long have you been a pilot?" Sean asked.

"Ten years," Kale said.

"Wow. Did you start flying when you were fifteen? How old are you?" Sean asked.

Grinning, Kale answered, "The ripe age of twenty-nine, I am. Should have started earlier because I've always loved the thought of flying. Dad wouldn't let me. Worried, I guess."

"Hmm. It's peaceful up here isn't it?" Sean rolled his head along the back of the seat and looked over at Kale, feeling more content.

"That's why I love to fly. It takes me away from the world below, away from all the crap and noise." Kale pushed the mic and headset to the nape of his neck, leaned back and relaxed.

They settled back to watch the changing scene, sun behind them setting while the dark sky became more evident up ahead.

"Do you like music?" Kale asked, tilting his head toward Sean.

"I do. Music would be nice. Are we allowed?" Sean said.

"I can do anything I want up here. What do you like?" Kale asked.

"Hawaiian music, I guess," Sean said.

"Ugh... Please. I can't listen to anymore ukuleles. Just because I was born and raised in Hawaii doesn't mean I listen to that crap," Kale said, grunting when he reached for the drawer beneath his seat where he kept the music.

"Sorry, I thought that was the only choice we had. After all, we are in the middle of the ocean with nothing more than coconuts and a few loose sticks to bang together, maybe a palm frond to shake." Sean laughed. "Now that makes some good noise."

"Listen. Not Nice. No making fun of my culture. Would you settle for orchestrated music?" Kale was already holding the disc and pressing buttons on the center console between them.

"Actually, I would," Sean answered, holding back a grin. He was warming up to the guy and his choice of music. He leaned back and waited for the music to start playing.

"Ah, this is nice, right?" Kale relaxed.

"Mm-hmm," Sean hummed.

"Hey, do you like chocolate chip cookies? I brought some." Kale leaned forward.

"Who the hell doesn't?" Sean answered, sitting up too.

As soon as Kale reached for the cookie box, he stopped and froze. His eyes went narrow and he listened.

Sean's face went flat. "What is it?"

Kale held up a finger, motioning for silence, lowered the volume of the music and pulled the headset over his ears. He glanced at the flight deck and saw the lights flicker, and then shot his eyes over at Sean and told him to make sure his seat belt was tight.

Sean sat firm in his seat, nervously checking that all the latches on the belts were in place and then groaned, "Oh, shit. What the fuck?"

Suddenly, the lights on the cockpit's panel went black and the tower's connection was cut off. Kale slowly pulled back on the throttle to slow the engines and tripped a dial that brought the plane lower.

The flight turned bumpy and everything inside the plane rattled.

"Hold on, Sean, it's going to get shaky, but we will be fine." Kale optimistically promised.

"Oh, Gawd." Sean turned cold, his fingers white from gripping the straps running down his chest too tightly. He chanted, "We're gonna die, we're gonna die."

"It's alright. I've got this. We aren't going to die." Kale pointed at a small island on their left. "Look over there. That's where we're headed. Just keep your eyes on that spot and you'll be fine."

All at once, the propeller's engine lost power and just as quickly regained it again. Sputtering and popping, the nose of the plane kept dipping.

Chapter 3

The lights in the cabin flickered, adding chaos to the already tense situation. There were signs of trouble, certain ones, and the way it seemed, the plane was going down with the two men in it. The plane rattled and the noise level increased.

Gripping the throttle, Kale did what he could to hold the plane steady, and hollered to Sean, "Under your seat is a floatation vest, get it out and put it on."

Sean's hands shook while he pulled at the safety straps that pinned him to his seat. Matters worsened as the plane tipped and dropped. Finally the clasp broke loose. "What about you?" he yelled over the thunderous noise.

Kale raised his voice, "I'll get mine, but first I need you to grab the throttle."

"What?" Sean shrieked, "I'm to fly this thing?" He looked at Kale, his face grimacing and turning paler.

"It's fine. Hurry. Grab the throttle with both hands and hold it steady. You got this." Kale crawled to the rear of the plane and lifted what appeared to be a large school pack, strapped it to his back and wedged himself into the seat behind Sean.

Sean snarled, "What the hell—are you jumping? Where's mine?"

"We both are," Kale shouted. "We can't stay here."

"Ho shit!" Sean groaned, then squealed when the plane popped and dropped about twenty feet.

Everything was moving faster, including the plane as it headed down.

Kale knew he was losing the flight; it was inevitable, unrecoverable at this point. He spun in the seat, feet to the window, and kicked it free. Instantly cold air shot through the cabin, bringing a hurricane-like storm with it. The pressure changed, sucking the plane to the left.

"Shit," Sean groaned again, trying to look back at Kale.

"We're fine. Let the plane go," Kale yelled over banging wind. "Spin the throttle to the left. Turn the plane out to sea, away from land."

"Why? What? What for?" Sean hollered back.

"It's alright. Just do it." Kale leaned over Sean, helping turn the throttle.

Sean growled as he spun the wheel, struggling to keep it turning.

"That's it. Good." Kale dropped back into the rear seat. "Get back here, Sean. Hurry. I need to strap you to my chest."

Sean grabbed his overnight bag and

shimmied backward until he tripped into Kale's lap.

It happened fast, Kale clipped the straps around Sean, securing him to his chest and then said, "Okay, this is it. We jump now or never."

The plane was falling fast, heading at an angle toward the ocean. The right wing dipped, forcing them to slide across the seat to the side opposite the escape window.

Still dipping, the plane rolled over, tossing Sean and Kale against the ceiling.

Kale drove a foot into the back of the front seat for leverage and told Sean to do the same while hollering, "Reach for the window. We need to get out now."

Sean kicked and growled.

It all just got worse. The engine sputtered, rolling the plane again, chaotically flinging them against the open window. Sean on top, crushing Kale against the fuselage. They were lodged, the parachute pack somehow hooked to the window casing.

Roaring and gripping the frame, Kale held on, his head out the window, hair snapping madly in his face.

"I need to unclip you," Kale yelled, and then did it.

Sean rolled off Kale, his legs spun wildly out the window and dangled there. Sean held on, eyes full of dread looking back at Kale.

Tugging, Kale pulled himself free from the casing. Taking less than a second, he spun his legs out the window next to Sean, hanging with him, then yelled against wind, "When I tell you to: let go. I've got you."

Sean couldn't speak, just looked at Kale, trepidation swallowing his once vibrant being, feeling death at his door waiting to take his soul.

Kale yelled, "It's not over yet, Sean. We jump together. I can latch on to you as we fall. It's the only way."

Sean nodded, praying still. His satchel and the life jacket fighting him.

Kale hollered, "On three, we jump."

Three came and they left the plane.

Screaming, Sean gave in to death while Kale scrambled to reach for him.

Sean clamped his eyes shut, blocking away the world that was spinning below him, but only for a second. "Kale," came out as a whispered plea, as if by saying his name kept him from falling to earth alone.

They whirled, dropping downward as the plane spiraled out to sea.

Chapter 4

While falling, Kale and Sean scrambled to reach each other, their hands meeting but neither able to get a good grip. The farther they dropped, the more terror lit their faces.

Sean's stomach churned, pumping an acidic lump to his throat where it stayed.

Kale reached and fought to grab Sean's hand.

Suddenly Sean's momentum broke, giving Kale a split second to connect and pull him to his chest. Within that same moment, the abrupt link tossed Kale to the right, pulling his grip on Sean loose.

Thrashing, Sean slipped free.

While somersaulting under and back over Sean, Kale miraculously caught him with a vice lock at his wrist, swinging Sean's feet far out to the side and back again.

Sean twisted and oscillated underneath Kale, hopeful his grasp didn't break loose.

Kale roared as he tugged Sean to his chest

where he held him tightly in his arms. "Dammit, I'm sorry, Sean."

Honestly scared beyond words, Sean grunted.

The wind suddenly shifted, aggressively thrusting them into a haphazard tumble, rolling them over and under each other. Again and again.

The shoulder bag attached to Sean turned violent, flipping up and then down, knocking into Kale. The punch to his jaw made him lose his grip on Sean again. Kale's heart sank as he watched Sean break free and fall, heading down while looking back up at him. Fear welled in Kale and the fight to catch his passenger escalated.

Kale pulled his arms to his sides making him shoot like a torpedo toward Sean. Catching up to Sean and speeding inches above him, Kale's hands clawed at empty space as he frantically tried to grab him. Over and over again he scrabbled, until one grip turned lucky and Kale got him by the hand. Intrusively, inertia barraged and as quickly as they locked fingers, Kale lost hold. Sean slipped away and as his feet flipped backward over his head, Kale threw his hand out snagging him by the pant leg, but force pulled at Sean and Kale couldn't hang on.

"This isn't happening," Kale growled, teeth biting down hard until his jaw ached. He roared to summon the strength he needed to get Sean back.

Sean closed his eyes and prayed.

At that moment Kale gripped Sean by the ankle, swiftly tugged him upward against his chest, scrambling with the clips that would keep Sean safe.

Thankful, Sean gasped, pulling air back into his emptied lungs.

"I've got you." Kale hugged Sean tight, pushing his cheek against his shoulder. "I won't lose you this time. I promise."

Falling still, Kale noticed the ground getting closer. He held Sean even tighter, squeezing him, hardly letting him breathe.

Their drop suddenly felt like a glide, almost tranquil. But soaring about five-hundred feet above ground meant chute release was crucial. Kale held onto Sean, jawlines touching.

"I've got you," Kale's voice lowered, yet was still loud enough to fight with pounding wind.

Stress bit at Sean's face, hampering serenity.

Kale warned, "I'm going to pull the cord in a second, so hang on to me tight. There will be an upward jolt and your legs will feel like they're being pulled to the ground." Kale looked him in the eyes. "You ready?"

Sean nodded, begging silently that the parachute opened.

"Hang on." Kale gripped the chute's rip cord and he tugged.

Chapter 5

The chute opened and just like that they shot upward while the rickety plane took a nose dive into the ocean a few hundred yards off the southern coast of Kahoolawe. On splashdown, it broke into what looked to be a million pieces. Their expiration would have been definite if they were in it when it impacted the ocean's surface.

When the parachute wafted to its fullest size, Sean grunted on the uplift, and his feet raised, swung around and then tangled with Kale's. He huffed when the chute finally settled, and he stared off into the distance, floating with the breeze, trying to find calmness after that riotous ride.

Kale had a sense of humor most of the time, quick-witted and smart. Even when the time for it wasn't right, he let go of remarks that demonstrated he had a carefree personality. "Well, that went better than expected."

Sean disagreed. "Fuck it did!"

"We're all good," Kale insisted, tugging on

the chute's right toggle to turn them toward land.

Sean held on, linking his fingers securely behind Kale's back and confessed, "Holy shit that was fucked up. Seriously."

"We're almost down." Kale pulled down on both toggles to slow the chute, making a go at a smooth landing.

With his back to their target, Sean couldn't see where they were headed. "Are we almost there?"

"Almost. Just hang tight and enjoy the ride," Kale said. "I am."

"Easy for you to say, you have a bird's eye view. And you said that same thing when we were fifteen-hundred feet above sea level. Everything about this trip across the sky was far from enjoyable, so until I'm on the ground, I can't just sit tight and enjoy the ride," Sean spit the words.

Kale laughed at Sean, even though he shouldn't have. He should have been as rattled as Sean, if not more. He had a life in his hands, a precious one and like any other pilot, was doing everything he could to get his passenger safely on the ground. That was one thing yet to do, land safely.

The smell of ocean salt was clearly in the air, telling Sean they were pretty close to a landing pad.

"Can you swim?" Kale asked.

Nerves rocking all over again, Sean rambled, "What? What the hell? What now? I need land! Get my ass to land."

"Take it easy. I've got this," Kale assured.

"I don't think you do," replied Sean, pushing away from Kale. There were only a couple inches between their cheeks, but it made Sean feel better to be even *that* far away from Kale.

"You'll be fine now. It'll be like landing on a cloud when you hit water," Kale said.

This time Sean ranted, "What? Hit water? Are you nuts? Get me to the dirt." He squirmed.

"You'll meet the dust soon," Kale confirmed. "Listen, either I drop you off here and let you swim to shore, or we both go down together and drown, your choice. But know this, two twin fishes can't successfully swim if they are stuck together."

"Just get me down, that's all I ask," Sean complained.

"That I can do but I need you to undo the clips so you can drop free." Kale nodded to Sean.

"You are nuts aren't you?" Sean argued.

"A little, but for now, do what I tell you so we don't crash and burn." Kale forced a smile, a calming one that would persuade Sean to do what was being asked.

"Oh, Lord." Sean found the clip at his left and banged on it.

"What are you doing?" Kale asked. "It's not a nail. You need to pull back on the lever to get it to release, not pound on it. What the hell?"

"I'm nervous, okay?" Sean reached for the clip again and pulled, lurching a little as that side of the vest broke away from Kale.

"You better speed it up. We're about a hundred feet or so above water with land not far ahead." Kale was watching Sean's hands shake.

"Shit, it's stuck, I think," Sean raved.

"Pull it, pull it, hurry, PULL," Kale screeched. "SHIT!" He yanked both toggles down to his hips, slowing the canopy as much as he could to avoid hitting water like a falling rock.

Sean failed miserably at freeing himself, never making it past the first clip. His heels hit water followed by Kale's toes, tugging at them hard and pulling them down fast, one on top of the other with the chute in tow. A warbled cry came out of Sean, and Kale yelled a gurgled 'oh shit' that was never heard.

Kale quickly let go of the chute's toggles and frantically tried to release the clasps that held them together so they didn't go under water any further.

His success with that was a problem because the wind kept filling the canopy and pulling them toward the shoreline. One good thing, they were headed in the right direction.

While being dragged, water arced over their heads, shooting a salty shower toward their feet until the momentum abruptly ceased and they lay in rolling waves where ocean met land. A less than perfect landing, but they were still breathing so that made it a successful one.

Kale huffed, gasping for air and then said, "Thank you for flying with Kale's Skyway. I hope you enjoyed your flight and we hope to see you again soon."

Spitting water, Sean pushed at Kale's chest. "More like Kale's collision. This isn't funny. I see no humor here. Now get off of me."

Kale pulled the levers on the last three clips that broke the connection between him and Sean. "You landed alive didn't you?" Without hesitating, Kale pecked Sean on the cheek with a watery kiss, pushed himself to his feet with a grunt and then offered a hand to Sean.

Reaching up, Sean took it, pondered a minute and then wiped his cheek where Kale had surprisingly kissed him. "What was that for?" he grumbled.

"What?" Kale asked. "I was helping you up."

"You just fucking kissed me. What was that about?" Sean grumbled some more.

"Relax. It was just a 'thank God we're alive' peck. No big deal, it meant nothing. I was thrilled to be safely on the ground. It was either kiss the dirty ground or kiss your dirty cheek. You were closer. You should probably think about doing it too."

"Kiss your cheek?" Sean pointed.

"No, chump, kiss the ground — be happy it let you back on it. Or what the hell — my cheek. Kiss whatever." Kale's hands went up and he turned an inviting cheek.

"Wow. You're full of it." Sean waded through the waves toward the beach.

"Hey wait up, get over here and help me take this thing off." Kale took off after Sean, tugging at ropes.

Sean turned back toward Kale, stretching his neck over the life jacket he forgot he had on. "Not only are you full of it, you're incredible with your demands, needs, and fucked up surprises."

Kale continued trudging toward Sean, picking at the shoulder strap and clasps that held the parachute cables to his back. "Hey there, I saved your tiny ass, the least you could do is help me out of these chains."

"You're relentless." But Sean was convinced.

"Get over here. I'm not coming to you."

Kale smiled, his bright teeth bouncing sunlight into Sean's eyes. "Not a problem. I can do that." Kale trudged through waves and stood in front of Sean at the edge of the beach. "You do the left, I'll take the right."

"Simple enough," Sean replied, hiding the onset of a smirk from Kale. He pulled the clasps on Kale's right and then pushed the strap up and over his shoulder. "Ya happy now?"

"I am." Shaking his left shoulder, Kale dropped the pack to the ground behind his feet. It limply floated up and over every wave. "Turn around. I'll help you out of that jacket."

"Hell no." Sean waved a finger. "After that kiss you snuck in, you're not getting anywhere near my ass right now."

"Right now?" Kale laughed. "What exactly are you saying? Does that mean I can go for it later?" He grinned.

"Again— full of it. Go ahead, get back there and undo the straps. No funny business." Sean spun around and let Kale take on the challenge. "Just so you know I'm not in the mood."

Kale unsnapped the catches while Sean lifted the vest up and over his head.

"What do I do with it?" Sean asked.

"We better hang on to it because it might be our only boat off this island," Kale said.

"What the fuck does that mean? Where the hell are we?" Sean ranted, looking around.

"Listen, chump, I couldn't exactly drop you off at Disneyland now could I? This was the best I could do at such short notice." Kale treaded out of the water and onto drier land.

"Stop calling me chump." Sean followed Kale.

"Will do, chump," Kale said it again and laughed.

"What did I just say?" Sean growled.

"That was the last of the name calling." Kale zipped his lips and continued further up the beach toward a sparse line of weeds about fifty feet in front of them.

"Do you have a clue where we are?" Sean asked.

"Yep," Kale replied.

"Uh, you gonna tell me?" Sean asked.

Kale stopped, huffed and faced Sean. "We landed on an island off the coast of Maui called Kahoolawe that at one time was used as a range to test bombs during World War II. There may be a camp of some kind still here for when visitors and hikers come to town. That's all I know about it. I don't think anything has been done with it since then. I believe it's still deserted because the ground is trash and isn't able to support much life."

"Well isn't this the greatest," Sean sarcastically complained.

"Like I said, chum... Sean, I couldn't exactly take you to a theme park with cotton candy and clowns. Now come with me and think of it as an adventure. Let's go, we need to take a look around to see what we're dealing with here."

Sean followed Kale like a lost puppy dog, drenched with salt water that left him soaked to the bone. Considering he just sucked out the window of an aircraft in midflight, freefell from the sky to what could have been his death, tied to an arrogant pilot who thought he had something funny to say about everything, and dumped on a deserted island with no food and probably no water, Sean was doing okay. A little pissy, but okay.

Chapter 6

Maui, their intended target was about fifteen miles northeast of where they were. They could see it, but didn't seem to have any way of getting to it.

Kale turned and headed back to the beach to get the parachute. The island gave the impression of being uninhabited, so it made sense to use the canopy as cover during the night if they needed to.

"Where are you going? Survival is this way." Sean pointed inland, away from the ocean.

"We will need a tent for the night. We're bringing the chute with us. It'll be perfect for shelter." Kale started rolling the canopy up before Sean came over to help him at the opposite end. They each made a tight roll, the two meeting in the middle, so when they finished, they were face to face, inches from the other, almost lip-locked and transfixed on each other's eyes.

Tension stirred in Sean and he quickly pulled away.

Kale reached for Sean's arm before he left.

"It's alright. We'll be fine." His voice went low and breathy. It was deep and sexy, and the way he spoke just then made Sean blush.

Kale finished by stuffing the canopy as best he could back into its storage pack and draped it over one shoulder and down his back. As he did he stood and waved for Sean to follow him down the same path they took a few minutes earlier. Traipsing, Kale whistled, like he was happy and content despite their current circumstances.

Happy? How could he be?

Moaning, Sean dragged his feet behind Kale as if he were on death row being led to the electric chair. "We are doomed. Oo-oh, we are doomed." He sighed. "Stranded on a deserted island, left to be eaten by wild beasts. Oo-oh, we are doomed."

Kale laughed at Sean. "We aren't doomed. However we might be stranded for a while. No need to worry though, the Coast Guard will be looking for us soon because they should already know the plane took off from Kauai, never reached its destination, and vanished from the radar. Believe me, we aren't doomed."

The sun was still up, but going down soon. They wandered through dry brush and weeds for what seemed like more than an hour, finding no life of any kind; not even a mouse or a bird. They came to an area populated with a few small trees. They were dry and most stood only knee high. It seemed to be the best spot they were going to find to take a break for the night. They needed to build their tent, dry out, and possibly get a fire going if they could figure a way to get one started.

Chapter 7

"We camp here," Kale gave the order as if he were a trooper of the tent brigade, inadvertently reaching out to stop Sean from walking any further.

"Here? In the dirt?" Sean argued.

"It's the best we've got," Kale said. "We don't exactly have many choices, this isn't a resort."

"What about rodents, snakes, and killer predators?" Sean mentioned. Glancing around at how desolate the place looked, he couldn't believe it was considered one of the Hawaiian Islands. They never showed sights like this on TV.

"There aren't any. Can't you see this place is too dried up to sustain anything living?" Kale gestured around where they stood, kicking at dry dirt, coughing when dust rose.

"Good to hear that bit of news. I guess that makes us next on the extinction list." Sean worked his satchel off his shoulder, swinging it around at his side.

Kale did the same with the chute pack, dropping it on the ground at his feet. He stood still for a few minutes, just looking at the sky; hot and stale, like they were in the desert someplace in the Middle East. "Do you have anything useful in that bag of yours?"

"This isn't a picnic basket, Yogi," Sean smartly replied. "I don't think there's anything in it that will make our stay better."

"Open it up, let me take a look." Kale reached out a hand. "There must be something in there we can use."

Sean swung the satchel behind his leg, hiding it. "There're just a few personal things in it is all."

"That's useable stuff. Do you have a lighter or any matches in there? C'mon, let me see. Why are you hiding it? This is survival. It isn't going to make a difference if I see whatever you want to keep hidden. I probably have the same shit. We're both men. C'mon, open up." Kale walked up to Sean, standing so close their lips nearly touched.

"Hold on." Sean nervously backed up, brought the satchel around and set it on the ground between them. He knelt down to unfasten the buckles and then went for the zipper that ran from one end to the other.

Kale knelt with him, scanning the bag to see what was in it. He grinned.

"What are you laughing at?" Sean said. "Look away."

"You." Kale turned his head toward Maui Island and then back at the bag right as Sean's hands went in it.

Looking down, Sean rummaged around

inside the satchel, quickly pushing the condoms and bottle of lubricant aside before Kale had a chance to see them. If it was up to Murphy's Law, the lube had already popped into view instead of staying buried at the bottom of the bag where he'd hoped.

Kale grinned after seeing what Sean seemed to be trying to hide from him.

Sean pulled out a book of matches, but unfortunately they were too wet to do any good. His one pair of underwear, shorts and T-shirt were just as soaked. "I told you, nothing," he said, waving the matchbook in front of Kale and then handed it to him, doing his best to distract the guy from seeing the tube of lube inside the satchel.

Kale took it, flipping it in his hand until it landed flat in his palm. "Alright then, since we're unable to build a fire, we'll just have to keep each other warm another way." He stood tall in front of Sean casting a shadow over him the same way a big-ass tree would.

"I'll be fine," Sean nervously answered, knowing what Kale was thinking.

"It gets pretty cool at night this time of year, and if you plan to sleep alone in wet clothes, you're sure to catch a chill," Kale said.

"I'm good, really." Sean zipped up his satchel and stood up. "Shouldn't you be worried about your plane instead of me?"

"There's nothing I can do about that plane and it's probably at the bottom of the ocean by now. My main concern is to get my passenger back to the mainland in one piece. If I have to lie on top of you in the dirt to keep you warm, I'll do it.

That's just how I am." Kale stood with his hands on his hips, trying to figure Sean out, wondering if he would like a set of strong arms wrapped around him during the night or not.

"Uh… Then you'll be cold and I'll be crushed," Sean said, feeling uneasy, moving a hand to rub his brow. "You look pretty heavy."

"Don't worry about that, we can trade places every so often." Kale laughed.

"Is that a joke?" Sean said. "What the hell?"

"It's a joke if you want it to be one," Kale said.

The beads of sweat on Sean's forehead made it clear he was stressed about sleeping with a man he just met. It didn't help any that his nerves were already beaten down by his fall from a fast moving plane.

Kale decided to let the sleeping arrangements rest, pulled the parachute from its rucksack and laid it out on the ground, kicking it a few times to give it some air, helping the thing open up and breathe a little. After a few kicks, Kale took off his pants and removed his shirt. The bulk of his chest and rippled abdomen came into view as the last bit of sunlight beamed over the front of him.

Sean presumed it was best not to gawk at the masculine beauty displayed right in front of him, but Kale looked amazing without a shirt on. Sean could see that even though he tried not to. The neatly trimmed short dark hair across Kale's chest played with Sean's mind, and he imagined what lay at the end of the hairy trail running down the front of his abdomen. If Sean kept looking, the swelling between his own legs would break free and expose itself to Kale in an obvious and embarrassing way. He stayed quiet and tried to be inconspicuous in his sexual fantasy, which wasn't easy. Then quickly looked away to camouflage the rising reaction Kale had lured out of him.

Damn that man.

"W… what are you doing?" Sean squealed.

"Trying to dry out." Kale stood only in wet underwear, all his goods outlined and on display in front of Sean. "You should do the same."

"I'm alright." Sean looked away, feeling awkward for staring.

"You can't be. You look like a wet chicken." Kale stepped over where his pants lay on the ground toward Sean.

"No, I'm all good. The wind will blow me dry." Sean inched backward.

"No, you're not good like that," Kale said, moving closer still. "Listen, I've been around here long enough to know that when the sun goes down the chill shows up quickly. You need to dry out before you catch that chill." He reached for the top button on Sean's shirt.

Sean grabbed hold of Kale's wrists and looked him in the eyes. "You seem to be in a hurry to get me out of my clothes. What's your game plan?"

"Would you relax, I'm just looking after you like a good pilot should," Kale said, wrestling with Sean's grip. "Your survival is still my responsibility."

Sean held on for a bit thinking the situation wasn't that bad. The man in front of him had the body of a military hero, completely his type. Kale was all solid, sleek muscle; with broad shoulders, a well-built chest lightly dusted with body hair that traveled down to a waistline that was trim and showed not an ounce of fat. From what Sean had seen earlier, the impressive outline beneath Kale's briefs was what he liked most in a man. He could tell Kale was very well-endowed but not freakishly large. He was also able to easily tell the crown of his dick was larger than the thick shaft that extended up and across his right hip. Sean swallowed hard as if the bulk of Kale's dick was already in his mouth and plunging its way down his throat.

"Uh... Hello. Are you going to loosen your grip so I can help you?" Kale said.

Sean nodded and then broke his grip on Kale's wrists. "Thanks for your offer, but I can do it myself."

Kale let go of Sean's shirt, backed away and returned to the parachute to shake it open further, laying it out to dry. It was their only cover, possibly their only bedding. While he worked the chute, he glanced over his shoulder a few times to get a glimpse of Sean disrobing. He liked what he saw when Sean was dressed, and couldn't wait to see what he looked like without his shirt and pants.

It didn't take long for Sean to be free of his clothes and standing a few steps behind Kale in only his Andrew Christians.

When Kale spun in the dirt, his eyes leveled with Sean's brief-confined dick. Not expecting Sean to be so close, Kale squealed, "Holy shit!" He didn't mind what he was facing, rather he enjoyed it; but quickly stood before he started sucking, a natural reaction for Kale when another man's dick swung into view only a few inches from his lips.

"Uh... Was that a good holy shit or a bad one?" Sean laughed at his own wittiness, loosening up a bit, finally becoming more relaxed.

Kale stuttered, "Um... a good one... I wasn't expecting you... uh... to be so close... but I'm glad you're here to help me with this."

Sean's laugh turned to a chuckle. "Yeah, sure."

Kale watched Sean, staring at his tight ass cheeks shifting from side to side as he walked away. "Holy shit, I'm fucked," he murmured, took a deep breath, and waited for Sean to reach the other side of the chute. Kale liked Sean's ass, his dick that had been conveniently in front of his face a few minutes ago, and the solid muscles that defined his chest and six-pack abs. The entire package Sean had to offer was turning him on to the point of giving him an erection.

Oh, Kale was definitely fucked.

After stretching the parachute, which practically dried while they lay it out across the ground, they rejoined each other and stared at it.

"Now what?" Sean spoke first.

"We wait?" Kale said.

"Wait for what?"

"Until it rises."

"What? Is that another one of your ridiculous jokes or is it really going to lift off the ground?" Sean turned to him.

Kale laughed at Sean.

"What is wrong with you?" Sean barked.

"The look on your face got to me. It was

classic," Kale said.

"I thought there was going to be some volcanic activity and that bitch was going to rise like you said. How do I know this shit? I'm not from around here," Sean squabbled.

Kale continued laughing, placing a hand on Sean's shoulder and squeezing.

"This shit you keep pulling isn't funny. Can't you tell that I'm stressed out?" Sean spun from Kale's grip and walked away.

"Okay, okay, no more funny business." Kale chased Sean, reached for his shoulder and turned him back around.

They met face to face when their bare chests bumped against each other, noses practically touching, their breath mixing between them. They both hesitated, looking into the other's eyes, then quickly parted.

Just like Sean thought, Kale's body was rock fucking solid, tight, and hot.

Splendid heaven, we're both fucked.

Sean stomped away in an aimless direction. "Help me find some sticks or something we can use to turn that parachute into a tent."

"That's not going to work. There aren't any sticks big enough on this nuclear-burnt island to make a tent tall enough to cover us." Kale followed closely behind Sean.

Hearing nuclear, Sean stopped abruptly and Kale bumped into his back. "So now I'm getting fried by nuclear radiation? This's great."

Kale gripped Sean by the waist, holding him in place. He liked the way his cock fit perfectly between Sean's muscular butt cheeks. "It was a long time ago when those bombs were tested here. All the traces of radiation are long buried by now, so you won't fry. Just your feet will."

"What? You idiot. Let go of me," Sean growled and pushed off of Kale.

"I'm kidding." Kale crept up behind Sean again.

"Are you going to help me find tenting sticks or what?" Sean threw out.

"We can look but the wind off the ocean will blow down any shelter we manage to build. We'll be better if we use the chute as ground cover and a blanket for the night."

"I'm not sleeping with you," Sean huffed.

"What's the big deal? We're just a couple of guys. Men sleep together in tents out in the wilderness all the time," Kale said.

"But they're dressed," Sean said.

"Not all of them." Kale smirked.

Sean blasted, "Let's just look for sticks, okay?" He stomped away.

Kale put a hand to his brow, shading the sun's last rays from getting to his eyes while he spun in circles looking for sticks he knew weren't there.

"What are you doing?" Sean asked Kale, watching him rotate in circles on one foot.

"Looking for sticks." Kale twirled with one hand still shielding his brow.

"You look ridiculous," Sean said. "Like a broken weather vane."

"There are no sticks on this bloody island. Let's just get back to the chute and make a bed out of it," Kale pressed.

"Alright, lead the way. This time I follow you." Sean sighed dejectedly.

"Fine with me. Surprise me back there if you'd like." Kale chuckled.

"What?" Sean snarled. "Get moving!"

Chapter 8

They crossed the dry land in silence, tension between them slowly mounting but under control.

They finally made it back to the "campsite" while it was still daylight, and noticed that in the short time they had been looking for sticks, the parachute had folded over like a taco shell with the top half snapping in the wind like a flag.

Looking at Sean, Kale waved with an open hand toward the chute. He didn't have to say anything because Sean knew what he meant by his sarcastic gesture: the effects of the blowing wind. *Told you so* was written all over Kale's smug face.

"Help me dig." Kale got down on his hands and knees like a dog and started pushing dirt back between his legs.

"A hole. Really?" Sean grumbled.

"Yes, a hole. I have good reason, now dig," Kale ordered.

They dug the hole until it looked like both of them could comfortably lie side by side in it. Then the chute went in, flipping one half of it over top of the other to create a pocket they could both slip into and rest.

"Why the ditch?" Sean asked.

"So the wind will blow over us. It'll help hold off some of the night chill," Kale answered.

"As long as it's not my grave site, then I'm okay with the hole," Sean pushed his hair away from his eyes, fussing and muttering the entire time, then brought his hands to his hips.

Kale laughed at Sean's theatrical gestures. "Grab your bag. We can use it as a pillow."

"We? There is no we." Sean's eyebrows furrowed. "That bag is only big enough for one head. Mine. You can make your own pillow with a pile of dirt."

"Are you always so dramatic?" Kale asked, tugging on one end of the chute while Sean got down and held the opposite end to pull it taut.

Sean sat back with his butt on his heels, hands pressing down on his thighs while he spewed. "Listen, I just fell out of a broken plane, landed in the middle of the ocean with man-eating sharks, traipsed across a deadly radioactive field looking for nothing, stripped down to my skivvies, and now am being told I have to sleep in the ground next to a man that can't keep his boner under control. For the love of Pete, I have every right to be dramatic."

Kale held out his arms. "Do you need a hug?"

"No I don't need a hug"—Sean stood, crossed his arms, looking angry—"not from you anyway."

"Drama queen," Kale whispered.

"I heard that," Sean yelped.

"Yep, you need a hug."

Sean growled, "Shut the hell up."

"There it is: drama."

Sean bellowed, "There's something seriously wrong with you, isn't there?"

"And more drama."

"Dumb ass!"

There was only a short time left before the sun set. The way it was going down looked as if it was falling from the sky, making nightfall feel like it was creeping in fast, which meant they better get their bed ready before the sky went black.

Their dynamic drop from the sky and the vigorous trek across what seemed to be desert-sands pushed Kale and Sean to the edge of exhaustion. It was only a matter of time before they collapsed from overall fatigue and hunger.

"Do you have anything to munch on in that bag of yours?" Kale asked.

"No," Sean flatly answered, dropping down on the ground, expelling a puff of air when he hit the dirt beside Kale.

"I thought I saw some mints or candy when you were trying to hide what you've got in your bag earlier." Kale motioned for Sean to get the satchel and check it.

"No candy or food of any kind in there," Sean insisted.

"Are you certain? I thought I saw something that looked like a candy wrapper," Kale pressed.

"There isn't. I should know." Agitated, Sean reconfirmed his statement.

"I'm pretty sure I saw something. Let me see the bag." Kale reached for it.

"For the love of my tight white ass, you're the pest of all pests, like a tick that gets under my skin." Sean grabbed the bag and tossed it to Kale. "Go ahead, see for yourself. No food will you find."

Blocking the bag from hitting him in the jaw, Kale raised his hands. It landed at his knees and his hands went after it. "Holy shit. There it is again: the drama." He unlatched the buckles and flipped the closure flap open.

"Pipe down and start your hunt for food. I hope you find what you're looking for, but don't be surprised when you reach for the golden wrapper and find that what's inside it isn't edible." Sean was sure Kale was up to no good and he had accepted that. Dread knotted his stomach a bit, but perhaps if he let Kale see the "treasure" he had inside the bag, he'd lay off all his badgering and go on being the savior he was supposed to be.

"Ah, found it." Kale pulled the wrapped morsels from the bag. "Oh." His eyes popped.

"Told you," Sean said.

Holding up the foil-enveloped condoms, Kale chuckled as he spoke. "Well these might be a bit chewy, but at least they will be long lasting and certainly won't go down without a fight. You'z a gum chewer, eh?"

A puff of laughter escaped Sean's gullet. He didn't mean to laugh, but he did. What Kale said was funny, and holding back would have only made him seem stuffier than Kale already thought he was.

"Such a class-A idiot." Sean grabbed the

rubbers from Kale and threw them back in the satchel just as Kale snatched another item from inside, the main product that most men and boys consider their first love. Lube.

"Cooking oil? This won't do much good if we have no frying pan or vittles." Kale was a smart ass for sure.

Not caring anymore and being blunt, Sean said, "You do know that's lube for butt-fucking and jacking your dick off, right?" He pointed at the black bottle in Kale's hand, hopeful he knew what he was holding.

"Really? No. Gee, thanks for filling me in."

At first, Sean couldn't tell if Kale was being honest about the lube as cooking oil comment or if he was actually having him on. But after the *'Gee really'* remark he was sure Kale understood the oil was to help make a dick penetrate a tight asshole with pleasurable ease.

"You've got lube too— real nice." Kale grinned. His body gave a longing shudder as he remembered using his oil-slicked hand to sensually stroke his dick and masterfully play in his ass. He almost went hard thinking about that and the times when another man's slippery dick pummeled him. He couldn't forget about the many times he rode a vibrating dildo or two either. Those were good times.

Oh Man!

Kale stared at Sean and wondered if he used the lube to fuck men and get fucked by men or simply used it to masturbate while he fantasized about men. Sean seemed like the versatile type to Kale and he was hoping he was a man's man and not one who thought of the ever dreadful lady bits. Kale shook his head a few times to bring himself back to reality, then handed the black bottle of lubricant to Sean so he could put it back in the satchel where it would be kept safe until it was needed.

"Are you finished horsing around?" Sean gripped the bottle and tugged on the bag Kale was still holding.

"For now. But keep that bottle within reach." Kale's smile went wide as he let the bag and lubricant go. The bottle was slippery so the release was effortless.

"Don't get your hopes up buster." Sean acted like he was offended by Kale's allusion, but he really wasn't. He truly liked the idea, wouldn't mind a one-or-two-nighter with a hot pilot. That was always a fantasy of his: the thought that if he was ever in a position to fuck one, he'd do it and it would be exciting. He found Kale reasonably handsome for sure and could easily take him on that night, but his scruples and rocking nerves were getting in the way.

Damn them scruples. Damn those nerves.

Chapter 9

Kale and Sean had nothing better to do than lie in the ditch and look up at the stars while watching the moon slowly move into position over them. Sean lay on the left, Kale on the right, both with their arms propped beneath their heads for that added comfort.

There were no words uttered from either of them as they lay next to each other in the ditch. Both were too whipped to move because it had been an exhausting day filled with physical and mental wear and tear. They were purely talked out and to move another muscle would have been torturous. The quietness that surrounded them brought isolation and peace and the safety of that made them sleepy. The only sound heard was the whisper of the wind and the waves rolling up and down the nearby beach. The tranquility of it all pushed Sean into a speedy slumber.

"Sean," Kale murmured.

Kale's masculine voice crept into Sean's

resting ear and stirred a warm pining inside him while he dreamed. It was familiar, achingly so, and a part of him wanted to snuggle up against Kale and fall sound asleep with the sexy, low lilting pitch wrapping around him like a comforting blanket. He wanted to pull Kale close, open up to him, invite the velvety heat into his core with slow clutching seduction, while another part of him screamed to turn away and tether his desires. He must have dozed off because the next thing he knew Kale was shaking his arm.

"Sean… You in there?"

Slowly waking, that low voice sounded good-humored to Sean, on the verge of a smile, and so sensual he felt himself giving up sleep just to hear it again. Then his eyes opened fully to the darkness and cold that had already moved in. Kale's warm hard body lying next to him made everything else irrelevant.

In spite of the darkness, Sean could feel Kale's eyes on him, tracing his torso from bottom to top, stopping when his gaze met his shining eyes. If his senses served him right, he could tell Kale wanted to kiss him, and if he was being honest with himself, he wanted that kiss to happen too.

"Wow, you totally went out the minute you laid your head back." Kale rolled on his side to face Sean, scooting closer, heat radiating from his bare chest.

"I'm exhausted," Sean slurred, his upper eyelids went heavy and fell to meet his lower ones, sticking together as if fastened with glue. Just like that he was asleep again, leaving Kale all alone in the dark.

It amazed Kale how somebody could simply lay back and drift into dreamland so quickly. He didn't have that pleasure. With him, it took hours before his mental lights went out. Much of the reason being he thought too much about everything he did that day and what he would be doing the next. It tormented him almost every night, going over and over and over every detail. Jacking off didn't even put his mind at ease, or relax him as it did almost every other man. He always thought he was cursed with insomnia or a restless syndrome of some kind.

After watching the stars drift across the sky for about an hour, Kale padded a few yards from the ditch to take a whiz. He figured if he couldn't sleep, he might as well get up and drain the main vain, or at least play with it.

While Kale relieved himself, the sound of it startled Sean, like he was hearing a horse urinating right there next to him. His eyes flew open—he hadn't realized he closed them—and felt heat climb his cheeks when he looked up and saw it was only Kale taking a piss a few yards away. The low rumble of a hose-like urine stream made him realize how endowed Kale must really be, much larger than he looked through his skin-hugging briefs. He was mostly a bottom man, so he liked a big cock. The bigger and thicker the better. Being a banging bottom who loved a big dick was kind of a package deal.

Sean rolled onto his side, facing away from Kale to avoid giving up how truly eager he was to see what was dangling between his legs. God forbid. Even though Sean wanted to explore every part of the pilot that dropped from the sky with him, take on the challenge of what sounded to be a sizable piece of meat, he made sure to keep his senses clear and hold his fantasies to himself. His asshole enthusiastically went on twitching to have every bit of that horse hung pole pummeling his rear end. He really wanted it, but the timing for doing it was way off.

Making every attempt not to disturb Sean, Kale quietly slithered into the ditch, taking the same spot behind him where he was before venturing out to pee. Moving slowly, he laid back with his shoulder lightly pressing against Sean's shoulder blades, just so he could feel he was there. The touch comforted him, felt nice to have another man lying next to him again, to feel the warmth of another body, making him feel less alone. Finally Kale's breathing went shallow and he started to drift off.

As Sean lay quietly awake, he could tell Kale was getting sleepy, legitimately sleepy. His difficult day of being a superhero had caught up to him. A few minutes later a faint, wheezing snore came out of Kale and he knew for sure the man behind him was out cold.

Halfway into the night, Sean was chilled, couldn't get warm no matter what he tried to do. He tossed, turned, rolled over and pulled his knees to his chest that put his body into a tight ball.

Kale felt Sean's restlessness as well as a cool sensation emanating from his flesh. He told Sean earlier he'd do what it took to help his distraught passenger survive, and if he needed to lie on top of him like a warming blanket, he'd do it. Kale was a hero like that, a good guy. He'd do just about anything to save a life. Kale rolled over, pressed his warm chest against Sean's back, wrapped his arms tightly around him and hoped he'd stay there in his arms. He sighed. Damn, Sean felt good in his arms.

There were a few shudders from Sean, chilled ones, before he settled down and started warming up again. Kale's cozy hug from behind felt comforting to Sean, a feeling he'd been missing and wanted to always come home to.

Chapter 10

There was a good share of angst that had built up between Sean and Kale throughout the day and for some strange reason seemed to pull them closer together. Even though it was the middle of the night, they were both wide-awake, and comfortable; lying in the ditch, one behind the other in the dark, neither one knowing if the other was miserable or content with their current situation.

For sure Kale had sensed tension from Sean all day long, but at the moment didn't feel any anxiety from him or detect any desire on his part to push away.

Sean didn't move, and lying with Kale helped him maintain a steady body temperature, no walking the edge of hypothermia anymore.

From behind, Kale held Sean the same way he did when they were falling from the sky, very close with a tight grip. He pulled Sean tighter against his strong body, feeling Sean's heartbeat through his hand fanned out across his chest.

Sean lay still, sensing Kale's erection crawling up his spine. He moved back, pressing his ass against Kale's enlarged cock. He wanted Kale to impale him from behind, wanted him inside to sooth his stinging soul.

Kale cautiously nibbled on Sean's ear, circling it with the wetness of his tongue. The warmth of his breath channeled over it and traveled down his neck. The sensation of hot and cold brought Sean's erection to total hardness, pushing his velvety crown above his waistband, on the verge of bursting with semen.

Fulfilling Sean's need from what Kale could tell, he moved his hand over Sean's chest, stroking one nub then over to the other. The sensual touches made a spark in Sean ignite, his back arched, grinding his ass harder into Kale's thickening cock.

Kale breathed and his voice went low, "Oh Gawd, I want to fuck you so bad. I've wanted to since the first time I saw you."

Wanting Kale more than he let on, Sean rotated in Kale's arms, facing him, their hard-ons sword fighting behind the fabric of their briefs and their lips close to touching.

Kale gazed into Sean's eyes and the sparkle in them instantly captivated him. He pulled Sean closer, crushing their chests even closer and their heartbeats jumped from one to the other.

Kale whispered while holding his gaze, "I need to kiss you, Sean." He held a hand to the back of his head, caressing and pulling him closer.

Sean's face went soft as Kale leaned in, then he stuttered, "I... I'm... " Lust for Kale blocked his thoughts and he couldn't speak clearly. He inched back and then lowered his lids.

Kale moved with Sean, hot breath glazing his skin, making him tremble but not pull away. Then it happened, Kale's mouth closed over Sean's, taking him over, giving him a kiss that was so tender and raw, yet somewhat sweet, a kiss that was pulled straight from his heart.

The contact was flawless and gentle, oh so perfect, and when the time came to separate, Kale nipped Sean's bottom lip as he backed away.

Kale's voice lowered to a whisper, "Now that wasn't so bad was it?" He held Sean still, caressing his jaw and then his bottom lip with tiny kisses, like little butterflies were landing and taking flight.

Once more, Sean's face went soft. He said nothing; he didn't have to. Kale felt his answer even before he asked it.

Kale blinked, leaned forward and softly pressed his lips to Sean's again, taking another sensual kiss from him and giving one back too.

Sean stirred inside and could sense a connection happening, like their souls were trying to unite. He pulled away conflicted with emotions as to how he was feeling. He was angry, sad even, a bit confused by his strong desire for the man who had put him in such a faraway place.

Sensing reluctance in Sean, Kale leaned in until their lips lightly met again. Sean's kiss was warm but his touch felt distant.

Sean stiffened and pushed away.

"What's wrong?" Kale whispered.

"I'm sorry. We shouldn't be doing this. I'm supposed to be upset with you," Sean said.

"Don't be," Kale said.

"I can't help it. I'm not happy about where I am." Sean started getting angry; his tone went up an octave.

Kale lifted himself up onto an elbow, looking down on Sean. "It wasn't something I did on purpose and this place isn't that bad. We have an ocean view."

Getting hotter, Sean raised his voice, "Is everything a joke to you? Fuck the ocean view; this is serious shit we're in."

Feeling the heat of Sean's temper, Kale jerked back and said, "Whoa cowboy, pull in the angry reigns. We'll figure a way to dig ourselves out of this shit pile we're in. We can look for shovels in the morning."

"More joking, you see why my ass is getting hot?" Sean rolled over on his back. "You can't make everything better with a clown act, Kale."

Kale laid back. "Okay. Done. No more attempts to make the shit we're in better by trying to find a bright side."

"Look around us, Kale. Look where we are." Sean crossed his arms over his chest. "I'm in a ditch with a pilot who can't fly a plane to save his ass."

"Hey, I can fly. It was the plane that decided it was time to call it quits," Kale argued. "And FYI, not only did I save my ass, I kept yours alive as well. If it wasn't for me, you'd probably be further down in this ditch than you are, with mud in your eyes instead of stars. You should be a little more grateful instead of a dramatic" — he paused — "bitch."

Sean sat up. "I'm a bitch because I'm fucking

angry, and miserable, and hungry, and tired. And fuck you, I am not a bitch."

Kale sat up, a little bothered with Sean, but he understood his anger. "I'm sorry, Sean, I shouldn't have called you a bitch. I didn't really mean that, it was the only word I could come up with on the spot. Let's just try to get some rest and we'll figure a way out of here in the morning." He pulled the parachute up and offered it to Sean, placing a hand on his shoulder, showing compassion. "Cover up so you don't get cold."

Sean pushed the chute away. "I don't want that fucking thing touching me. It's colder than the bloody air."

Kale scooted closer to Sean, wrapped an arm around his shoulders and rubbed the chill away. "Then take my body. It'll keep you warm."

"I don't want that either," Sean lied.

"Yes you do, and there it is: the drama." Kale grinned. "I know you want it."

"Fuck you!" Sean squealed, nudging Kale with his shoulder.

Kale pushed Sean to the ground on his back, climbed on top of him and pinned him with a kiss. A good one that shut him up for at least a few seconds.

A cross laugh escaped Sean. "Can you get the fuck off me, please?" He struggled with the weight of Kale on top of him, punching playful fists against his chest.

Kale fought back, grabbing Sean's wrists, pinning them above his head. "Calm down and I promise I'll let you go."

"Alright. Just get the fuck off me." Sean

settled a little, but he remained restless.

Kale loosened the grip he had on Sean's wrists, backing away slowly, ready to grab hold again if Sean started swinging. "We good?" Kale sat up, towering above Sean while saddle striding his hips, feeling Sean's erection coming to life.

"Yes. Good. Can you get off me now?" Sean pushed his palms against Kales chest, helping him move.

"I'm staying, and that's final." Kale didn't move off him, but rotated his hips to make Sean hard.

Sean saw Kale as a stunning man, so brutally masculine and powerful; he seemed too statuesque to be real. Kale's beauty was more than Sean could take and there was no stopping the reaction it had on him. Sean pinned his eyes to Kale's muscular chest, fascinated all over again by its strength and the soft dark hair that spread across it like tiny feathers. His hands caressed and petted, watching it expand with each breath he took. Visually inspired, his eyes traveled further, following the trail of hair lining his abdomen, moving on to the lump inside his briefs.

Holding back no longer, Sean drew Kale down against him, quietly lying in the dim moonlight, embracing and kissing, letting their erections battle. A deep timbered moan rattled from Kale's chest as he felt Sean's erection move side by side with his.

Betrothed with Kale's gentle but masculine touch, Sean grew harder, reveling the hair on his chest which he liked so well, warming him, scrubbing sparks of pleasure through his perked up core.

Kale removed Sean's briefs, exposing his cock, examining its beauty as it slumped densely up and over his left hip, taking Sean in his hand and squeezing. Enthusiasm struck Kale, and like a wild bull, his thickened dick broke free of his own briefs, landing heavily on top of Sean's.

Observing Sean's body, Kale ran eager hands along the gutter of his abdomen, and over his thickly muscled chest. "You're so beautiful, you know that?" He leaned in, kissing Sean again, receiving his piercing tongue.

Sean moaned, getting harder still.

Kale twisted each of Sean's nubs, first the left, then the right, making Sean whimper, wanting more. Slowly, so slowly, he ran his hand further along, stroking the deep impressions of Sean's abdomen, stopping when he met his dick. "Can I fuck you?" Kale muttered, his warm breath caressing Sean's mouth.

With their lips still touching, Sean reached above his head for his satchel, blindly searching for the rubbers and lube. "Yes, fuck me, now," he demanded.

Kale dived deeper into Sean, kissing him hard with a rotating jaw and chewing mouth. Kale's breathing went sharp as he eagerly sucked on Sean's tongue.

Kale's hand feverishly gripped their erections together, squeezing and stroking in his tightened fist. Rocking back and forth, Kale's stiff cock stroked Sean's.

Sean sensed Kale's meaty dick pulsating against his, cocks burning together in the heated stroke of his hand, gliding from base to tip. Pre-cum oozed out of Sean's narrow slit, giving Kale the bit of lube he needed to keep pumping.

Sean's body temperature rose with each kiss Kale left on his chest, his nipples, his ears, and along his neck. Pleasured cries escaped Sean and the sensation of a climax seized his body, the intensity growing inside him. Sean craved Kale badly, wanted and desired him, needed him to make that ultimate connection, to fuck his begging hole.

Anxiety spread in Kale, the desire to fuck Sean overpowered his ability to hold back. He thrust uncontrollably, breaking the fisted grip he had on them.

Sean's hard-on jumped as he watched Kale position himself between his open legs and coat his wrapped erection with a lubricated hand, stroking himself, making his cock stiffer for Sean.

Sean quivered when Kale's oily hand brush up against his greedy entrance, slicking his hole, getting it ready for the beastly invasion.

While Kale stroked himself with one hand, his other punched a pair of fingers right inside Sean, thrilled at the way his tight hole gripped the two digits sliding within. It was warm and tight, and so inviting. Sean groaned, begging, needing more.

Kale sensed Sean wanting to be stuck for good, not with just a few fingers, but with his slippery enlarged dick. Sean's actions were clear, and from that, Kale gripped himself and aimed his glistening fuck-post at Sean's flexing star.

Pulling his knees to his chest, Sean exposed

his begging entrance to Kale, aching to be pummeled. Needing it deep.

Taking the lead and teasing, Kale punched his shining hood against Sean's manhole, tapping it softly, just breaching the seal. Then giving more, Kale pressed harder at the same time Sean eagerly pushed back, sucking him in. Kale's bulbous cap burst through Sean's ring, plunging deep inside him until his entire cock was veiled.

Buried deep in Sean's ass, Kale's rhythm was on fire. He rocked into Sean, grinding, circling, pulling out and digging back in again, making sure Sean was satisfied as well as himself. Revealing his yearning to get closer, Kale nuzzled Sean's neck, licking and kissing it, while rutting in and out of his contracting hole.

Sean's pleasured whimpers turned louder as Kale bore down on him with his fervent cock and tongue. His legs locked tightly around Kale's hips holding him securely to keep him close.

Kale kept up his rhythm as if matching a drumbeat, banging, pumping, thrusting his cock in and out of Sean's sucking chute. It felt like hot pleasure to Kale. Hot, cock-pounding pleasure. Rough and dirty for their first time fucking.

"Fuck me harder! Pound my ass! Faster!" Sean ordered domineeringly like a bossy bitch, his legs spreading wide now.

Kale reciprocated without protest, pounding into Sean, shoving his dick deep, drilling him into the ground with his power-driving dick. The satchel at the back of Sean's head boogied along with Kale's body, keeping perfect rhythm to his wild thrusting.

"Holy fuck your ass is fucking sweet," Kale groaned.

Hypnotized by Kale's ball busting intrusion, Sean's mouth sprung open and he could only whimper.

Kale stared down at Sean, watching his reaction as his thick, pistoning dick probed and jolted that sweet spot inside him.

Sean gripped his own cock, jerking it with a tightened fist, tremors netting him inside the growing orgasm sparking within.

Seeing Sean convulse beneath him was all Kale could take. He pushed his cock in until every large inch reached for Sean's chest, groaning with desire each time he felt Sean take him in, his ass sucking on his dick in a starving manner, pulling Kale deeper inside.

Kale pumped his hips into Sean like a madman, banging into his ass with the speed of a jackhammer, his dick getting sucked and stroked beyond the point of no return. They moved together wildly, friction building, bringing their massive explosions to the brink of release.

Possessing Sean, madly kissing him with rising desire, Kale hummed broken words into Sean's ear as he started to tremble on top of him. "Are you ready"—he groaned—"oh Gawd"—he huffed—"for my load?" His face turned to a pleasured knot, but he didn't stop fucking.

Sean's orgasmic pleasure made him struggle answering. "Mm-hmm,"—he whined—"shoot me." The friction inside Sean made him lose all control. That sweet spot was being bumped again and again. He jerked and jolted as his own hand-cranked orgasm bubbled up and shot from his dick, spraying streams of hot semen between their chests, soaking them with soaring ribbons of cum.

The pungent scent of Sean's sperm fanned over Kale and because of it, the extraordinary orgasmic buzz overcame him too. He bleated and blasted, blowing sizzling semen up against Sean's bowels over and over and over again, filling the condom to the point of bursting, stretching it to the max.

Sean went warm as soon as he felt Kale's vigorous cum pump inside him. It was like a drug, a sedative that helped him meet his calm.

Surrendering to his orgasm, Kale lay over Sean tightly against him, sensitive and trembling.

Their mouths met, inhaling each other's breath until their convulsions settled. They kissed as their passion turned from roaring lust to sensual and tender, slowly regaining self-control.

Oddly and suddenly, Sean laughed. He couldn't hold back his emotions. He liked the position he was in, with a handsome pilot on top of him, but that wasn't the way he had imagined this day would end.

"What's so funny?" Kale sniggered, keeping his cock where it was, gently moving his hips in small circles.

"I'm sorry about that. I can't believe all that's happened today and it ended with you — the guy I resented earlier — cock-fucking my ass. Don't get me wrong, I enjoyed every minute of it, and you were good at it, but if I may speak honestly, it all seems so twisted, and the thought made me laugh." Sean squeezed Kale's shoulders.

"That's a relief. I thought my fancy fucking made you crack." Kale went back down on Sean, locking lips.

Sean took hold of Kale's tongue with his and mumbled, "Nope."

Still hard, Kale pushed his hips into Sean again, going as deep as he did before.

Sean's eye lids fluttered and his head fell back when Kale's talented erection hit the magic spot inside him again. "Ho fuck, that's awesome." He gasped.

"Next time you can be on top." Kale's voice was deep and sexy, but an intrusive grunt followed when he grabbed Sean's shoulders and rolled him over.

Sean looked down into Kale's eyes and every thought about him being exiled had vanished.

Chapter 11

An hour of fucking in the ditch on a deserted island was physically arduous and neither one of them noticed the strain it put on their bodies until it was over.

Sean collapsed and rolled off of Kale, gasping.

Kale laid there breathing heavily, waiting for his erection to relax even though he would prefer it still tucked up inside Sean's sweet, tight hole. It felt so much better there.

Finally settling down, Sean lifted up on his elbows, looking at the stars. "That was an awesome fuck, a great ending to a fucked up day."

"Glad to hear you liked my dick up your ass. It was good for me too," Kale said, propping an arm behind his head, seeking stars with Sean.

Sean inhaled the salty air while glancing down at Kale's dick, kind of letting out a disappointed sigh that it was not still sliding in and out of his ass. The beast lay stiffly up the center of his six-pack abs, tucked comfortably in his cum-gutter, but was slowly working its way back down to a more reasonable size. The fucking thing impressed Sean, it was huge. He always loved taking on a sizable challenge, but that fucker? Holy shit!

"What are you looking at?" Kale rolled his head toward Sean, the sparkle in his eyes almost blinding him.

Sean nodded toward Kale's cock. "You plan to keep that thing on?"

Kale looked down at his big boner wrapped in rubber and laughed. "Oh shit, that's right. Go ahead, do the honors."

At first Sean glared at Kale, but then thought what the heck; another challenging bicep workout today might be good for him. He sat up completely and stared at Kale's dick, nestled comfortably in the dark hair above it, not too sure he should disturb its slumber. "You sure loaded that thing up," Sean said.

"Your sweet ass made that happen. I couldn't hold back," Kale confirmed. "Aaand, I probably could have kept going."

"Aaaand more humor." Sean reached out and gripped the base of Kale's heavy dick with one hand while his other slowly, so slowly slid the condom along its length, pushing it over the head and off where he dangled it between two fingers over Kale's chest. Frothy semen clearly filled half the condom, and the weight of it all stretched the rubber downward like a water-filled balloon.

Kale squirmed beneath the swinging ornament as if he was offended by it. "Back off with that thing beeyatch!" He pushed Sean's hand aside and the cum-loaded condom swayed back and forth, looking as if the bottom of the low hanging rubber was ready to burst.

After glowering at each other, Sean said, "What's the big deal? It's your spunk."

"Really. No big deal, huh?" Kale clapped his hands over the dangling condom and the cum inside shot up and out of it like the spurt of a fountain. It shot everywhere. Onto Sean's face, Kale's face, dripped down Sean's chest and somersaulted into the hair on Kale's. It was quite a display and a pungent one too.

"Fuck my butt, you asshole!" Sean quickly stood, let go of the condom, dropping it with a splat onto Kale's chest.

The second it hit Kale, he jumped to his feet and the condom flipped from his chest and landed on Sean's foot with another squishy splat.

Sean screeched, kicking the wet rubber over Kale's ducking head and the wiggly thing ended up in the dirt somewhere behind him.

"Hot damn, you should be on the soccer team," Kale acknowledged, standing up and then laughing about the flying rubber.

"Enough horse play. Hand me my underwear so I can clean myself up," Sean said, wiping cum off his cheek with his hand.

"Then what'll you sleep in?" Kale asked.

"Nothing I guess. It doesn't matter. There's nobody on this bloody island anyway and you've seen my best parts, which not many people have the pleasure of seeing, so naked isn't going to be any surprise to anybody here," Sean licked his lips.

"Oh, Gawd, I just tasted your cum."

"Lucky you, how was it?" Kale sniggered.

Sean licked again and confirmed, "Mmmm, not bad."

"I guess that means you won't go hungry," Kale said.

"Oooo, good idea. It's supposed to be nutritious." Sean furrowed a brow, the left one.

"That can be plan B, or A, whatever." Kale reached for Sean's briefs with his toe and tossed them across the ditch.

Sean caught his underwear with one hand, wiped his face and chest before tossing them to the ground and commented, "Fancy footwork. You should consider joining the soccer team with me. You're talented in so many ways."

"Yep, that I am. Be right back, I need to pee." Kale found a quiet place about ten paces from the ditch where he could piss in private. No need for an audience even though his only viewer had a bull's eye view of his pecker a few minutes earlier. Utter relaxation of releasing the flood gates came to him, and while waiting to finish pissing, he brushed a hand across his chest and spread cum there into the hair on it. He'd done that before and worked perfectly in a pinch.

While Kale was out taking care of the business of his bladder, Sean realigned the ground cover and put the satchel back in place for his head. Exhilaration from having a handsome pilot up inside him on a Hawaiian beach made him smile. Actually he beamed.

Returning from his break, Kale spotted Sean lying in the bed they made together, he radiated, happy to see him there and couldn't wait to snuggle with him. They both needed it and what better way to end the day than with a comforting hug.

Sean stared at Kale as he walked his way, gazing at every part of his muscular frame, from his sculpted face to his sexy toes, becoming more obsessed with what he saw and never wanting to miss out on any of it again. Wonder seized Sean when he saw the massive meat that dangled freely between Kale's thighs, amazed that something so glorious existed and that he was able to take the entire thing up his ass without flinching. He'd thought it before, *but seeing that fucker? Holy Shit!*

Smiling, Kale slid in next to Sean, meeting face to face. "Okay my tight-assed lovely, we need to get some sleep." Kale inched closer to Sean, pressing their bodies tightly together, locking lips for another kiss.

"You better be referring to my buns of steel and not making a statement that pertains to cheapness and beauty?" Sean spat, tugging at the back of Kale's hair.

Kale reassured him, "It's all about that ass." He gave it a pat and a squeeze.

"Saved," Sean mumbled.

"You can tell me how tight mine is next time." Kale smirked.

"I so look forward to that." Sean rolled over on his side and tucked his rear end into Kale's warm groin, it was hairy and cozy, the way Sean liked it to be. Having Kale's oversized cock parting his bare butt cheeks and running up his spine was comforting. He liked that too, in fact, he loved it.

Kale cradled Sean in his arms, tightly spooning him, one hand locked around his wrist and the other fanned out across his chest. He held him close, very close from behind, nuzzling his cheek against Sean's ear and whispered, "Good night, Sean. See you tomorrow."

Without giving a second thought, Sean rotated his head back and kissed Kale, like they were long time lovers. "See you in the morning, my sweet, sweet fucker."

Chapter 12

Sean opened his eyes to see Kale leaning over him with a sun-made halo behind him. He lay in the shadow cast by Kale, hearing the water splash in the surf and some other sounds he couldn't quite identify.

Kale leaned in and kissed Sean, brushing his lips with his tongue before parting them and going inside.

Despite his recent orgasm, Sean's shaft tried springing to life at that intimate kiss, twitching as Kale tongued and sucked him gently, holding onto him for an endless moment before disconnecting.

The lust from the previous evening left him and Sean grumbled, "Oh Gawd, what have we done?" He tossed the back of his hand to his forehead and then dragged it down over his eyes, blocking out the sun and Kale's halo. Apparently the thing they did together last night—Sean couldn't quite bring himself to call it making love because it was more like lustful sex—didn't seem to bother Kale at all. Maybe Kale was used to one-night stands with strangers, banging assholes and butt fucking at first sight? Sean didn't think of himself as being like that, so he pushed him away. He had scruples, so he'd thought until Kale came along.

Kale didn't know whether to be relieved or irritated about that reaction. Then again, Sean seemed to be blessed with principles that Kale did not. To Kale the sex they had was supposed to be a practice run so to speak, like many others he'd had, but with this guy, Sean, he wanted to go for another practice run, and possibly another after that. He liked Sean, felt good being with him, drama and all. Could it be Kale was getting emotionally invested already? Within a few measly hours? Was that even possible?

Sean sat up, looking at Kale with one sunblind eye, the other clamped shut in order to block out the blazing sun. It was so damned bright and he wasn't ready for so much light to be invading his space just yet. He brought his knees to his chest and said, "I hope you don't think I'm a slut. I never, ever spread my legs and fuck a guy on the first date."

Ignoring the mention of Sean being a slut, Kale inquired, "Is that what that was? A date?" His hand found Sean's thigh and he rested it there.

Sean fussed where he sat, straightened his legs out in front of him and did a one-eighty from what he first said, "Noo… No, no. I meant to say, on the first night, like a one-night stand. That was no date, definitely not a date. Please."

Kale's hand did a sweep across Sean's thigh

and he moved it to his shoulder, squeezing it gently a couple times, the effort subtle. A smile took over the corners of his mouth and before he could filter his thoughts, he said, "I would have been happy with it being a date, Sean." When he spoke, his voice was surprisingly sexy. Deep and convincing. And it got Sean's attention even before he finished saying it.

"More like a bad beginning to a rocky romance." Sean's face went long after he realized what he just said, used the word romance when he probably shouldn't have. Another slip of the tongue — Freudian-like. Perhaps that's what he really meant; he subconsciously wanted to get a romance started with the man who fucked him during the passionate clutches of the previous night. He went cold and stammered, "Forget I just said that. Wipe it from your mind." He stood up and crawled from the ditch, looking intently out across the ocean.

"You're hooked on me, aren't you?" Kale followed him.

"What?" Sean shrieked. "You're nuts."

Even though they started off rocky from the outset, they seemed to be a good match, complimenting each other's strengths and pacifying each other's weaknesses. Aside from the bantering back and forth the way old married couples do, the tie between them was turning into a very short tether, getting tighter by the minute.

"You could say that. Nuts about you," Kale said.

"I changed my mind. You're crazy, completely mad. I never should have let you stick your dick in me." Sean stomped across the dirt toward the open sea, still naked, holding his junk in place to prevent racking and wrenching the best part of him.

"Where're you going?" Kale tramped a few steps behind him, naked too and carrying his treasure in *both* hands. He had to; great endowment comes with a heavy price.

"I need to get off this fucking island and away from you," Sean roared.

"You can't. We're stuck here... for now. Make the best of it."

"I'll swim to shore. I can't stay here another second." Sean kept walking, picking up his pace until his strides became a run.

Kale watched him go, knowing he wouldn't get far.

Sean kept going until he was waist deep in water and the waves pummeled him back toward shore. They beat at him; he tripped twice, once rolling forward and again falling back before a bigger wave enveloped him and pulled him under.

"Fuck. Damn you, Sean." Kale took off running after him, figuring the man couldn't swim in Hawaiian waters. The biggest waves on the planet graced the islands and could without a doubt take out an elephant. He sucked air and dove in after Sean.

Sean's head surfaced, coughing and flapping every limb in an effort to stay afloat. When the wave receded, he finally stood and said, "What are you doing here? Let go of my ass."

"I've got your ass because it needs saving." Kale roughly towed Sean backward toward shore, one hand on each hip, like he was going to fuck him from behind.

Sean propelled his arms in midair, like he was trying to fly, or swim, or whatever. The truth was, he wasn't going anywhere, not without a boat and a paddle. That was a no brainer. "Let me go. I can swim," he said.

Kale kept tugging and said, "No you can't. It's too far."

Losing his balance, Kale fell backward, Sean landed on top of him before rolling to one side where he just laid there, crumpled like a fetus, wanting to puke up the ocean water he'd swallowed and scream out of pure frustration.

Sean was angry, hungry, thirsty, and frustrated. He stood and began walking in a circle, stopping after about the tenth rotation, and blurted out, "Is there a God?" His arms went up and he looked to the sky, waiting for his answer.

In a deep voice, Kale thundered, "I am here with you, my dear Sean." He almost laughed.

Sean dropped his arms and turned toward Kale and bleated, "What the fuck? This isn't funny!"

Placing saluting fingers against his forehead Kale said, "Sorry, no more. Scouts honor."

"You said that before," Sean disputed.

Kale figured Sean was more upset at the whole stranded on a deserted island thing than at him, so he ignored his tantrum. But the fact was they were stuck on that island. Kale knew how these things worked, rescues with downed aircraft; if the ATC were tracking their flight as they should have been, they'd be out looking for them soon, if they weren't already searching. With that in mind, he was able to hold onto his sense of humor about the whole thing and keep hoping for the best.

A hug and a song had been known to calm rattled nerves, and as recently witnessed; Sean seemed to have lost his shit and needed a hug and maybe a song as well.

Kale wanted to help Sean relax, take a load off, but wasn't sure which one of the two methods would do the trick, singing or hugging, so he did both. It was the only way.

Holy crap it was working.

Sean swayed with Kale and said, "I'm starving to death."

"We'll eat soon. Look a boat," Kale kidded.

Spinning around, breaking free from Kale's hug, Sean looked for the rescue team Kale just mentioned and rattled, "Where? Where is it? Where is the fucking boat?"

Oh shit!

Kale regretted what he just said, but was only trying to lighten the mood. "I was kidding. No boat."

"Damnit... Kale!" Sean's heart went into overdrive, beating so hard it turned his whole body into a bass drum. He could feel it pulsating everywhere, toenails to skull. He twisted his head back at Kale, chest heaving, teeth grinding, hands pressed against his temples. "Fucking hell, what is wrong with you? I... Shit... I mean... Fuck... Are you a fucking... Shit, shit, shit... Is everything a joke to you?"

Kale couldn't accuse Sean of being dramatic this time because he had earned the right to be on stage pulling drama duty right then. So Kale just stood there and stared, waiting to be hit with a ballet slipper or a balled up fist.

"I can't even look at you right now." Sean boiled.

"But…"

Sean's finger went up, not the bird one, but the pointer. "Cool it. Not a word." He glared at Kale and then turned to face the island of Maui that looked no further than a bunny hop away. So close, but yet so far. If he reached out a hand, he could almost touch it. He dropped to the dirt and sat there, hanging his head, disgusted with his situation and a bit angry at Kale for putting him there. It wasn't totally Kale's fault, but he needed to blame someone. Too bad for Kale, it was he who flew the fucking plane.

Sneaking up next to Sean, Kale plopped down beside him. "You mind if I sit here? It's lonely over there."

Sean looked at Kale broodingly and answered, "I don't own the place, so feel free to sit wherever you want." He wanted Kale to pay for lancing his hopes of escape, but the guy was probably already feeling remorseful for the position he sort of got them into. There was no reason to twist the dagger or push it any further into his flesh than it already was.

Silently they sat, listening to each other breathe, neither one saying anything that might possibly upset the other. Sean drew Xs and Os in the dirt with his finger, Kale drew hearts and arrows.

Kale spoke first, grunting as he stood.

"Maybe we should have a look around, see if we can find something to eat. I'm hungrier than a bitch."

Sean peered up at him with the famous one eyed look.

Holding out a hand, Kale helped Sean up. Locking his gaze, hoping to rebind the tie that felt like it was about to snap. "Let's get our clothes. They should be dry by now."

With a pissy grin, Sean said, "I have dirt in my crack."

"No big deal. We can work it out with a few splashes of sea water." Kale laughed, brushing Sean's bum. "After you, we can do mine."

Sean's smile returned, a little gritty, but it was there.

Chapter 13

"Do you hear that?" Kale stopped dead, his pants clinging below his thighs.

Sean didn't seem to hear anything, or maybe he was tuning out Kale's stupid humor. It wasn't a good time to be falling for anymore of his fucked up horse play. Sean zipped his pants, ignoring Kale. It was over, kaput, he'd had enough. No more tricks.

"Shush, really, do you hear it?" Kale hummed again, quietly cinching the belt around his waist.

Sean stopped breathing and said, "You better not be fucking with me."

"Not this time. Shh, quiet." Kale placed a hand over Sean's mouth.

Sean grimaced at that. Under any other circumstance being bound or gagged would be fun, but this time it annoyed him. His expression quickly changed to one that was more wondrous and he mumbled, "What do you hear?"

Tilting his head to one side like a dog does when it hears a high pitched whistle, Kale toiled at honing in on the sound he thought he heard: that of a boat engine. It had to be a big one, like a ferry or hopefully a Coast Guard vessel. "It's over there. Lets go. Hurry."

Sean sprung to grab his bag in an automatic reaction.

Barefoot and half-dressed, they speed-walked up the coast. That walk quickly turned into a run as the sound of the boat became more apparent. If ahoy was still part of the sailor's vocabulary, they would have certainly yelled it out.

The agony caused by the thought of being left on that dried up island washed away at the site of the red and white rescue boat. It was real; not an illusion or a mirage, nor another one of Kale's sickening jokes, but real.

"It looks like a rescue boat, right?" Sean managed to lighten his spirits enough to think more clearly about his and Kale's predicament.

"Thank the fucking stars, it is," Kale pronounced, tugging Sean along his side by the wrist.

They hung out along the coast, jumping up and down in the surf, waving their arms above their heads to get the attention of the rescuers. As soon as they spotted a blinking light directed at them, they settled on their knees in the wet sand and wheezed.

The same way a dog chases its tail, the vessel circled the surf, creating more waves that rippled toward the beach. The boat rotated another time before powering down and floating as close as possible to shore.

Kale and Sean both could feel their whole fucking day was about to get better. It had to. No ifs, ands or buts about it. Time had come to end this miserable trip.

Chapter 14

As the Coast Guard vessel rocked with the waves near shore, a handsome crew-member bound in an orange floatation jacket and a smile as wide as the bow on the boat helped them aboard. Kale, being the gentleman that he was, positioned himself behind Sean and pushed him up the ladder with both hands on his ass, copping a feel, just like old times. Kale followed Sean up the ladder, letting handsome hold his hand.

Kale then towed Sean away from the boat's side rail by the arm, gripping his wrist so hard it almost hurt, his thumb sweetly rubbing up and down the tender artery along the inside, possibly out of guilt for making him feel pain.

Joining them at the middle of the top deck was the handsome gentleman who helped them aboard the boat a few minutes earlier. The man noticed the affection between Kale and Sean, and either ignored it or thought nothing of it. He carried with him two life preservers, one for Kale and the other for Sean, and told them to put them on so they could get the boat underway to the mainland.

As soon as the watercraft started moving, the engine's noise level lifted, making any attempt at conversation pointless, unless they yelled. Nobody felt like yelling, so talking during their quick ride to the island of Maui was only to tell the officer on board that they were indeed the survivors of the plane crash they were out looking for. The only two who had been on board the flight.

With his satchel pinched between his feet, Sean sat quietly beside Kale, shoulders touching, letting him do what little talking there was.

The perfect gentleman supervising their boat ride to Maui figured Sean and Kale were a couple. He apparently saw them as sweet and thought they looked good together. He smiled a couple times, hoping they noticed that showing their affection for one another was fine with him.

When they reached Maui, there was a car standing by at the mooring dock for them, presumably in position to take them to the building across the parking lot for questioning. The vehicle looked certified, shiny white, with a Coast Guard seal marking each front fender and one on the plate pinned to the rear. It was official. The investigation of the crash had begun, and Kale and Sean were lodged right there in the middle of it. They were actually the main subjects of the entire investigation.

Sean's corporate run to the Hawaiian Islands wasn't supposed to turn out the way it did; getting mixed up in a plane crash, treacherous skydiving tricks, official investigations and shit.

Added to *the shit*, was his concern about his reputation at his workplace. They probably thought he made a new life in Hawaii at their expense. All thoughts along that line would be nullified if he was able to make a phone call, send a text or email. But for reasons known to him, he was being prohibited from contacting anyone. He couldn't just pick out a pigeon and tie a note to its foot. There weren't any birds on that blasted island he could have made his personal messenger anyway. If his office only knew he was stuck on a deserted island, his worry over their thoughts of him as a deserter would be eased. All he could think about at the moment was getting his ass to a phone or computer in order to do the imperative: make that call so they knew he hadn't abandoned them.

In Sean's opinion, the company he worked for was partially to blame for what had happened. It was their idea to put him on that cheap-ass plane instead of one that would take him from point A to point B—safely. They should have paid more attention to the service being offered instead of the discount they were probably getting. The only good thing that came out of the whole crappy flight /crash/near-drowning/deserted island fiasco was meeting one hot pilot and getting fucked by him. He was feeling the resulting muscle aches caused by the positions he held while being plowed in the ass by a big dick.

Kale spotted the concern taking over Sean's face and asked, "You alright?"

"Yeah, I'm fine. I think everything just hit me

is all... I need a phone." Sean coughed as if that would help get rid of the feeling that an infestation of bugs were crawling around inside him.

The car rolled up to the building that was close enough for them to walk to, but the Coast Guard had their procedures, which included taking them there on wheels, so no one questioned it.

"Follow me, and these shirts and paper slippers are for you to wear." The man from the passenger seat slammed the car door behind them after Kale and Sean got out.

They shuffled their paper covered feet through a brightly lit hallway to a small conference room where one big ass table sat in the middle surrounded by about two dozen chairs. It was a claustrophobe's nightmare for sure.

Kale rubbed his chin between his fingers and thumb until red streaks started to show. He looked like shit. Sean did too, but not as scruffy.

The atmosphere in the room was like pea soup, thick and foul, and the overhead lighting even made it look green.

Through all the questioning, which came at them very mechanically—almost clinically, Kale groaned and rolled his eyes in mock disgust. They had so many questions for Kale, who truly would have liked to have had all the answers. But he just didn't. He couldn't pin any of it down, and told them so, but figured it was engine problems, so he stuck with that. How the hell would he know what the problem with the plane was? He's no aircraft mechanic, just a fucking pilot. There was no reason for directing most of what was being asked to him since he didn't have the answers they needed. He continued giving them what he thought they needed, or wanted to hear, until they let up. The one thing he made sure they knew, however, was the location of the plane; figuring if the bitch was located, hopefully in retrievable condition, his story that he didn't purposely bring it down would be confirmed and he could collect insurance on the bastard quicker and easier.

Finally being released from the interrogation pit, which is what it felt like, Kale rejoined Sean in another part of the building that looked to be a preparation kitchen for the residents who pulled all-nighters. It was big enough for that. The place reminded Kale of a firehouse where the ambiance emitted brother-hood.

Sean was sitting quietly, waiting, and it appeared they were done with him long before Kale's release because there was a pile of empty peanut packets that could have fed twenty or more mice crumpled in front of him. A sure sign he'd been sitting there for more than a few minutes.

"Gawd, I'm glad that's over." Kale walked up behind Sean and squeezed his shoulders with both hands, trying to break the tension that had cramped his mood. "Everything go okay with you?"

"Yeah. Good. They didn't ask me much, just wanted to know if you had been under the influence of alcohol, drugs, or some other weird shit that made your vision blur." Sean stared into empty space in front of him.

"Did they give you your one phone call?" Kale humored him, adding light through the fog that seemed to be billowing around the room.

"They did and you're still an idiot." Sean grinned, knowing he was trying to be witty.

"All good then? For now?" Kale asked.

"Mmm-Hmm," Sean breathed.

"Did you get hold of your office?"

"Yep. They flipped out but were sincerely concerned. They told me to take my time getting back and when I was ready to get on another plane to give them a call and they would make the arrangements," Sean said. "They're even taking care of my room and board expenses here until I feel ready to return."

"I like that idea. It'll give us a little time together in a civil setting." Kale smiled.

"Are we free to go? What did they say about that?" Sean spun in his chair and looked up at Kale.

Letting go of Sean's shoulders, Kale said, "Yes, we can go soon. They asked us to wait here a bit and will come get us when our rental car arrives. I used their phone to make arrangements before coming to get you."

Sean stood up, brushing peanut crumbs from his lap and said, "Good deal. I don't know about you, but I sure could use a power wash and a whole lot of food."

Kale laughed. "I'll join you. But first, let's see if they'll let us use a computer so we can find a place to hunker down for a few days."

It was one hell of a long day that led them well into the afternoon on Monday. After their unexpected adventure that started the day before, they definitely deserved a hot shower, a load of food, several alcoholic beverages, and one comfy bed for some recreation, rest and relaxation.

Chapter 15

They found a quaint place in the hills to stay, a bungalow instead of a hotel. It was one of those home exchange deals where the owners swap houses for a period of time during a holiday break. Nobody was occupying the home at the time, so it worked out perfectly for Kale and Sean.

As soon as they were checked into the home, cleaned up and dressed in the new clothes they picked up on the way over, dinner plans were being settled.

Kale was more familiar with the island than Sean was, so he took the wheel and led the way. This time if the engine decided to give out, one good thing was they were already on the ground.

They rolled into the restaurant a few blocks away from where they were staying, one that served fare typical of Hawaii, including alcohol served in pineapples. It was a charming venue; outdoors with an ocean breeze, doused with all the Hawaiian flare they expected, including a flowery lei that looped their neck.

While tilling through the traditional Hawaiian dinner, ground fire-roasted pig and a few mind relaxing drinks, they carried on with several conversations about nothing, the boring get to know each other ones, mostly blah, blah, blah and more blah, blah, blah.

The one thing that stood out during their chit chat session was when Sean said, "You should have asked me that last night before you stuck your dick in me and pounded your way to oblivion."

That wasn't the answer Kale was expecting when the question was, "So what brought you to Kauai?" But really wanted to know, so he asked it again.

Sean didn't mean to avoid the question the first time, his response was what came to mind at the time and he thought it was funny, so the second time around he answered, "I was there on assignment to decorate a new summer home for a client who lives in Madrid, the guy's loaded with money, and wanted me to be his personal designer."

"Wow. Special." Kale sucked on the straw poking out of his pineapple drink.

"That's what I thought and I was honored. Out of all the people this man could have chosen, he decided on me. Sure I have a special talent for interior design that comes to me naturally. However, those at the office seem to think he hired me because of my mug shot that I included in the packet sent to him, not basing his decision on the talent displayed in my design images alone." Sean smiled coyly, though honestly.

"You're handsome, Sean. I don't blame him for making a decision based on your face." Curiously Kale tilted his head. "That's all he got out of you, right? He's only seen your face?"

"That's cute," Sean said. "If I screw around with my clients, it literally fucks shit up. So I don't do it."

"Just your pilots?" Kale mentioned in all fairness, his brow furrowed.

"Not fair. I was vulnerable, feeling lost and alone, not myself and you know it," Sean countered.

"But it was good, yes?"

"Meh."

"What the hell?" Kale blurted.

One side of Sean's mouth went up, smirking and he added, "Well... actually... it was one of the finest fucks I'd ever had. Truly. You were a master. You certainly know how to work that dick of yours."

After that comment, Kale was unable to hold back his ear to ear grin. It thrilled him to hear what Sean just said about his masterful ability working his dick in and out of him, because he had truly been trying to give him his best, reaching for his heart, making sure he sent him over the moon so he'd come back for more. "I've gotta say, you brought that out of me."

"I have that effect on men,"—Sean's face changed to arrogant—"happens all the time." He back-flipped a hand in front of him.

Kale's ears pricked and then he prattled, "Anyway."

"Relax, I'm kidding. I told you, I'm not a

slut," Sean reminded Kale.

"You were one last night," Kale countered. "But... I didn't mind. Nope, not at all."

Sean grinned and suddenly his tone of voice stiffened. "I don't usually lunge at men like that, please know that. We were alone in the dark, practically naked with erections that could break stones. I was hot and bothered, so to speak; a bit because of anger, so I figured what the hell, may as well fuck the guy and make my shitty situation a better one. What more have I got to lose?"

Kale leaned back in his chair, his fingers tapping a rhythmless beat on the table top but before he had a chance to respond to Sean's comment, hot steaming cups of espresso were served, bringing the evening's dinner to its final stage.

Sean scooted closer to the table, ready for that caffeine pick me up and said, "Everything's going to be okay now. I can tell."

When Kale downed his last sip of espresso with a hissing slurp, his face appeared to be shutting down, eyes fogging over, looking a little glassy. He'd had a heavy couple of days, so it was no surprise that a wave of fatigue was coming over him. It'd only been a single night, but sitting at the table next to Sean, Kale felt a yearning within himself for the guy, a need to tell Sean how he was feeling, what was on his mind, and that he wanted to see more of him, much more. Kale felt like a bleak void had pried his chest wide open at the realization he may never see Sean again after that night. He couldn't let all his hope and happiness be sucked away so suddenly. He put a hand over his eyes and fought back the headache that was desperately trying to turn into tears. He wasn't usually that fragile, hell he was always tough, but he felt a strong connection to Sean and it was cracking his heart, punching a big black hole in it. He took Sean's hands in his and squeezed, not caring if anybody at the restaurant noticed. The only thing louder than the persistent heartbeat in Kale's ears was the sound of Sean's shallow breathing.

Sean quickly noticed the change in the air surrounding their table and took a moment trying to intuit Kale's thoughts, finally waiting for him to say something. Anything. At All.

Afraid of what Sean's response would be, knowing it was probably going to hurt like hell, Kale asked it anyway, "After tonight will I ever see you again?"

That was a loaded question Sean wasn't prepared for, but he answered, "Gawd, I want that. Really I do. The shit we've been through has definitely bound us together for life, probably had something to do with fate. That will always be there. Can we just get through tonight?"

Kale's macho exterior was crumbling. His eyes misted over and his throat was getting tight. A sure giveaway as to how he felt. He chugged water like he was dying of thirst. The chilled water made his throat better but didn't help his heartache.

Chapter 16

The drive back to the bungalow after dinner was quiet, neither Sean nor Kale spoke much, actually both hardly said anything at all. The air inside the car was thick, like most of the oxygen had been sucked out, making it harder to breathe.

Sean sat back in the passenger seat, thinking about all the kind and tender words Kale said at the dinner table that made his heart swell one minute and nearly break in two the next. There seemed to be so much Sean liked about Kale, but was there enough there to keep him interested? Sure there was the danger, the outstanding sex, but that wasn't all he wanted in a relationship. There were so many more pieces to a successful, long-lasting partnership. Sean wanted a settled life, a ranch style home with a yard and a dog, maybe a horse and cat. Kale seemed to be the opposite of that, the penthouse type that had a fifty story view, a bit on the wild side, dangerous, carefree and jovial. Maybe that was good for Sean? Something he could live with, a complete opposite. Maybe not? Sean wasn't the type who invested in anything unless there was some sort of guarantee, or at least an inkling of one. If only he lived closer to Kale or Kale to him, everything would be so much easier. Sean kept thinking about going the distance with Kale, a man he met just a short time ago who entered his body by way of lust, but he kept shifting his thoughts to "What if." Like getting the relationship going and then discovering it fizzled because they didn't have enough in common.

Kale looked across the car, reached for Sean's hand and brought it over to his thigh beneath the steering column and kept his on top of it. He told him, "I can hear those wheels spinning. You shouldn't be thinking shit that might not make sense."

Sean stopped himself right there, put a stop to the turning wheels Kale was able to somehow see, squeezed his steely thigh and said, "Listen, I like you. I know it's strange to be saying that so soon, for me anyway, but I have fears of falling apart because I based my infatuation for you on a thrilling skydive and an awesome fuck job. Do you know what I'm talking about?"

"I do. I guess." Kale rubbed the back of Sean's hand with his thumb and then linked their fingers together in a man-loves-man grip. "Look, we'll spend the next few days together, explore bodies and minds, then see if you still want to make a go at being together. You don't have to make a stay-or-go decision right now."

Sean brought his other hand over and clasped all three together, sandwiching Kale's in the middle. "That decision should be made by *us*, Kale. It shouldn't be me, or you, but *us*.

"Okay then, *us* it is." Kale smiled, feeling he was getting somewhere with Sean. He needed to because he liked the guy, everything about him including all his flipping drama. "We can do this, Sean. I want to. Look what we just survived! God knows we've been through tougher times."

"That's a damned fact." Sean laughed and tenderly kissed Kale on the cheek, for the first time thinking of him as a boyfriend when he did. He could really care about this guy, and if he was truly being honest with himself, it kind of scared him. He'd never felt so strongly about anyone, and certainly not someone he just met the day before.

Chapter 17

The minute they stepped through the door of the bungalow, Kale dragged Sean directly into the bedroom. He actually had other things planned; romantic things, but at the moment was thinking less about romance and more about fucking around with Sean again, like dipping his dick in the honey pot or vice versa. Kale's cock was aching and had been the entire ride home, there was no time for flowers and romance, he needed to bed that man, fuck him and be fucked.

"You're in a hurry," Sean shuffled in Kale's grasp.

"Shut up," Kale snarled. He pushed Sean down on the bed and released his wrist so he could strip him of the new shirt he had on. A few buttons flew as he tugged it up and over Sean's head, he didn't give a shit, he just wanted Sean naked. He ran both hands over the hard, muscular planes of Sean's smooth chest, reveling in the masculine feel of his body. Even though he *was* a bit of a drama queen, the guy was fucking virile. Kale gently pinched Sean's nipples, then leaned in to lap at one until Sean hissed, pushing his chest into Kales mouth for more.

Sean gasped while Kale slid his tongue across his chest, stopping to nip sharply at his other golden nub, lapping it gently to ease the sharp pings of pain. Sean's body buzzed and he writhed under the pleasurable assault to his chest.

Kale also whirled from the effects Sean's earthy scent had on him. His mind already associated it with fucking him. It reminded him of the same pleasing fragrance that dominated his senses the first time he filled Sean with his cock, fucking him until Sean's body took his cum. That was the scent he would always remember and hopefully have the pleasure of breathing in every night and day.

Pulling away from Sean's nipples, Kale stripped him of his pants and underwear, leaving him totally nude and vulnerable, lying across the bedspread. Kale licked his lips and said, "Gawd, you're fucking beautiful."

Kale toed off his shoes, tugged his own shirt up over his head and dropped his pants. He climbed on top of Sean, straddled his hips and settled in like that, with their cocks grinding into the other's, Kale's pressing down on Sean's.

Sean reached down between them, wrapping his fingers around both their erections, slowly stroking from base to flaring head, pre-cum beading at the tips.

Looking down, Kale admired the way Sean's muscles shifted as he writhed beneath him on the bed, loved the way his hair lay in disarray across his forehead, his lips slightly open, moaning and panting. But most of all, at that moment, Kale loved the feel of his thick cock in Sean's hand being stroked.

Sean regretfully let go of their dicks, he had to or they would both cum and the fun would be over. He moved his hands to Kale's chest, massaging the hefty masses that felt like iron, hair tickling his palms.

Kale's eyes closed and then slowly opened, the pleasure of Sean's hands making contact with his chest sent electric sparks through his body, putting him in a spiraling bout of ecstasy that wasn't quitting any time soon. He leaned over and kissed Sean, long and slow, just like he'd been dying to do all evening. He parted Sean's lips, feeding him his slippery tongue, then pulling back he said, "Tonight's your night, Sean. I want you to fuck me, and fuck me good."

There was no question in Sean's mind that he wanted to stick his cock inside Kale, and with those words, his heart leapt, and his dick jumped, pressing harder up against Kale's. "How do you want me?"

Kale pecked small kisses along Sean's jaw, stopping where ear meets skull and whispered, "I want you just the way you are."

Chilling shockwaves of pure desire raced up and down Sean's spine as he thought about penetrating Kale's hot ass.

At last Kale drew back and reached for the tube of lube and condoms on the nightstand beside the bed.

Sean's cock was stone hard and standing straight, pointing to the ceiling. He nodded and waited patiently for Kale to roll the rubber down his full blown shaft. "Gawd, your hands feel good," he moaned.

"Just wait 'til you feel my ass." Kale eagerly grinned as he rolled the condom on, taking his time. He repositioned himself over Sean's hips, at the same time tucking a lubricated finger into his tender entrance, then two, and then three. He shuddered from the exquisite torture of his own fingers relaxing his tight star, gently scissoring inside himself, anticipating the feeling of Sean's cock gliding in instead.

Sean watched Kale work himself with eager hands and then said, "That's nice, open up for me, but not too much, I like it tight. I want you to really feel me."

"Get ready, Sean," Kale groaned, his eyes fluttered when he punched his prostate.

Sean started stroking himself, running a slick hand up and down his shaft, the pleasure was painfully intense. "Fuck Kale, I feel like I'm gonna explode if I don't get inside you soon."

Then Kale leaned forward and kissed Sean, ravishing his mouth with passion, and when he rocked backward, he impaled his burning channel on Sean's rigid erection, slowly, inch by inch. His body trembled when his ass cheeks met Sean's thighs, taking his dick all the way inside. Kale squeezed hard as he rose and lowered himself again and again, stroking Sean's cock, making the man beneath him squirm, making him want to cum. Kale bounced up and down on Sean's erection, deliberately rubbing the crown of his dick over the sensitive spot tucked inside himself. Kale whined and roared as he slid on and off, the intense pleasure ruining him, making him quake.

Sean fought back the urge to cum as he gazed up at Kale, watching the muscles across his torso roll and flex as he took that ride on his rock hard dick. Sean moaned, letting Kale's channel grip and pull him in.

Wholly satisfied, Kale rode that dick, squeezed it, sucked it, and held it in. His mouth sprung open and uncontrolled moans erupted, getting louder, pushing his growing orgasm to the brink of igniting.

"Oh my Gawd, Kale," Sean whined. "We need to stop for a bit or I'm going to cum inside you right now." He gripped Kale by the hips, holding him steady.

With his cock still throbbing angrily, lying hard against Sean's six-pack, leaking pre-cum, Kale forced himself to hold still even though every cell of his being had cried out for him to keep riding.

Sean pinched his eyes shut to help dampen the sensation of his increasing orgasm, hoping to make it cease. He pulled Kale to him by the nape of the neck and kissed him. It began innocent and sensual but soon ignited to fevered osculating, rotating jaws with penetrating tongues.

By itself, Kale's burning channel flexed and sucked on Sean's erection, eagerly trying to pull semen from it, craving it, like his body needed it to survive.

The heat in the room was intense and Kale really wanted to get fucked. Not made love to, not gently caressed, but really fucked, hard and raw, like only two men can. He made a snap decision, spun around on Sean's hard-on, faced his feet and pulled off his dick with a pop.

Sean's thick dick, hard as stone, flipped back against is abdomen with a thud. "Fuck, what's happening?" He gasped, lifting his head from the pillow, spotting Kale's asshole aimed right at him, flexing and begging to be invaded.

Kale balanced on his hands and knees, like a saw horse, turned his head back toward Sean and ordered, "I want you to use my hole, fuck the hell out me. No mercy, just drive it in and fuck me senseless. Come on, get on me. I need your cock shanking me — bad."

Sean quickly got to his knees, then lined his cock up with Kale's puckered hole and drove it inside him, to the hilt, as far as he could go until the hair above his dick scrubbed Kale's cheeky orbs and stopped him from going farther.

Kale's body pulled him in, sucking on his cock all over again, madly craving his sperm.

Sean pushed forward while holding Kale firmly in both hands by the hips, their hardened thighs crashing into each other's, balls bumping too.

Kale pushed back, pulling Sean's extended erection in. The sensation was dirty. It was amazing. He howled, groaned and even grunted.

Sean bit his bottom lip, pulled back and pushed his hips forward with a hard grinding grunt, savoring Kale's pleasured reaction as he accepted all of him.

Kale shook with unrestrained enthusiasm as

Sean's thick cock drilled into him, pulled out and shoved back in again. Together they moved in perfect rhythm, rocking, pumping, pushing and fucking.

Sean bore deep, very deep, hiding his cock to the root. When he felt Kale's ass contract, he slid all the way out and held the crown snuggly against his shining star, teasing him, wanting to hear him beg for more before giving him back his cock.

It worked, Kale cried out for it. "Shove it in, Sean. Fuck me. Gawd please. Fuck my ass hard. Please." Kale pushed back when he felt the emptiness, pulling Sean's stone hard cock back inside him again, taking every inch, putting it back where it belonged.

"Fucking hell, that's nice." Sean watched his dick disappear, and then picked up his pace, plowing Kale harder, in and out of his sweet gripping ass, pummeling him like he wanted. "Milk my cock with your ass, Kale. Make my shooter cum inside you."

The dirty talk triggered Kale to go wild. He cried out, "Fuck my hole, Sean. Stick my butt with your huge cock. Keep going." He thrust back and forth over Sean's dick, pulling off it and then making it go back in.

Sean's face knotted, he groaned, "Hot damn. I'm gonna cum soon, Kale." The onset of his orgasm wracked him. "But I need to see your face and I want to kiss you when I do."

Even though Kale was having the time of his life being fucked on all fours, he was more than happy to flip over and see his new boyfriend from his favored position, on his back facing his fucker.

He rolled over and gave Sean a lopsided grin, spread his legs and said, "All yours, Hun."

Sean moved forward on his knees, grabbed Kale by the ankles and spread his legs wide open. "Damn nice. You sure have a hairy fuck hole," he commented, breathing heavily as he brushed the crown of his dick through that hair and pressed it against the entrance that so eagerly wanted him back inside.

Breathing hard, Kale said, "Can't help that. I'm all man. Don't you like it?" He pulled one knee to his chest and let Sean hold his other.

"Gawd no, I fucking love it. Helps me find my target." Sean popped only the head of his cock inside Kale, pumping small jabs back and forth at first before plunging all the way in.

Kale screeched when he went in, "Fuck me-hee-ee!" Then his head slammed backward into the mattress and his mouth flew open, panting from the thorough pleasure of being plowed by somebody he could love.

Sean thrust into Kale, again and again and again, punching into him hard and then slow, changing the speed and power of his talented thrusts. He didn't want to stop, he wanted to stay where he was forever, to seal the deal and make Kale his. He plowed into him even harder when he felt the surge within him surfacing.

Kale watched Sean's magnificent body move above him, taking every bit of him in as he bore into him. He let Sean use his body to get off, love it if he wanted to, and at the same time allowed himself to enjoy the wild ride.

Sean gave up a rhythm of fast, deliberate,

deep thrusts, pounding hard against Kale's sweet spot, over and over again, coaxing his orgasm to release.

Both moaned and groaned cursing with intense pleasure the other was giving.

Sean fucked Kale's willing body and huffed out, "Fuck, I'm close, Kale, you?"

Feeling the tidal wave of pleasure coming, Kale's mouth blew open silently, he couldn't speak. He gripped his cock and stroked it, nodding to Sean that he was about to burst.

They both roared and their bodies convulsed as if on cue. Sean kept fucking, building momentum as they both reached the pinnacle of release.

Sean bared his teeth, roaring as his face contorted into something savage. The second his pelvis buzzed and shot electric shocks up his spine to his brain, he collapsed on top of Kale and ravaged his mouth, kissing him in a beastly manner, sucking and blowing air like a wild bull. He dug into his mouth seductively with his tongue while he blew load after load of hot cum into the condom up Kale's fiery chute that was still contracting and flexing around his cock.

Between them at the same time Sean was emptying inside him, Kale's world rocked too. Hot semen from his dick shot clear to their chins and over their shoulders, some making it past their heads. Hot semen oozed down Kale's ribs and plastered areas of Sean's chest.

From their previous engagement, Sean knew Kale was a big producer, but what he saw then, outside of a condom, blew his mind and he was far from being disappointed.

Sean continued kissing Kale, still twitching from the final orgasmic surges, and Kale kissed him back with utmost meaning.

With his gasping settling back to a normal breathing pattern and his heart rate slowing too, Sean collapsed on top of Kale and hugged him. Quietly he whispered with labored breaths, "You are so damned amazing in the sack, Kale. That was another memorable fuck I'll never forget."

Eventually their breathing evened out and a sleepy desire came over them.

Settling into Sean's arms Kale asked, "What happens tomorrow morning?"

Sean nibbled Kale's lips. "You get to fuck me."

Chapter 18

It took less than forty-eight hours for Kale and Sean to realize they were a match made out of heaven. They started out on the rocky side, but that could be what made the last few days so intensely sexy between them. They each had a quirky side that the other didn't agree with, that's normal and who doesn't, not everybody can be one hundred percent compatible. A true fact of life and they both knew that.

A few days had passed and like new companions, they probably stuck their dicks in and out of each other so many times that they lost track and should be content with the game of sex well into the next Christmas season. They christened the entire house, every bit of it, including a few places outdoors, like on top of and under the patio table, and as they balanced in a swinging hammock. That was tricky, so many holes to slip a dick into, but they made it work.

Regretfully, the day of separation had

arrived. Neither one wanted that day to come, but unfortunately it was inevitable.

The alarm clock quietly buzzed right on time. Seven in the morning was early but gave Sean time to get ready for the flight back home to Los Angeles, including another ride on a pilot's dick before departure.

Sean nudged Kale a few times to get him to wake up. The weight of Kale's body on top of him had pinned him in place and he could hardly move. Sean's right arm was asleep, buzzing and floppy-limp, but he dealt with it and mumbled, "Kale, get up."

"What the–?" Kale slid off Sean's chest and sat up, rubbing his eyes like a little boy. The morning sun glared through a nearby window, hitting him in the face like it was a blazing flame thrower.

Sean kicked the bedcovers from his feet. He gripped his still full-blown erection, holding it against the center of his abdomen while he waited for the swelling to go down. It didn't. He pulled his pants on at the same time he heard Kale sleepily ask him to get back in bed.

Sean tripped over a few misplaced items on the floor as he made a crooked route for the bathroom to take a much needed whiz.

Kale dropped back against the pillows, tossing his arm across his forehead to block the intrusive sun beams pushing through the window next to him.

Sean peeked at Kale around the door frame right before closing the door and saw him holding his erect cock in his hand, straight up toward the ceiling. The damn thing was huge and always looked like he needed a ladder to climb it when it was hard. Sean liked that about Kale, among many other things. Kale was attractive in the nude, Sean could see that clearly, and the sunshine touching his soul made the man light up like a stone cut god.

Kale stroked his erection a few times, making it more difficult for Sean to resist and hollered, "Come back to bed. I'm steel stiff and you're the only one who can relieve me of this misery that's purely your doing. Get over here and take a seat."

Sean needed it again, wanted his pilot inside him. He wouldn't allow any reigns to hold up a great ride, so he hurried back to bed and claimed his seat. "Ho, fuck, you feel good. I'll never tire of having you inside me, Kale."

Kale cradled the sides of Sean's head, looking at him, deeply, almost through him, watching his face as he slowly slid inside him. Kale's jaw clenched and he pushed himself a little deeper.

Sean gasped as Kale entered him slowly and then confessed, "You're so damned beautiful, Kale, everything about you. I can't imagine not having you in my life."

Kale loved hearing that no matter how many times Sean said it. At that moment he needed to reach the furthest depths of Sean. He had to; he was falling in love with him. He bucked his hips once, one good hard thrust, impaling Sean, shoving his dick all the way inside him, going for his heart.

Sean's ticket home to L.A. was waiting for no one, so their sexual escapade had to be quick this time. It started out slow and heartfelt, then went to a mad and explosive place like most of the other times they'd fucked, then turned to a slow love session that thrived on kissing, caressing, entering each other with soft rhythmic rolling hips, trading places, and pleasing each other lovingly. Then the cum spurted, oozing everywhere, like ten men had been in the room with them, soaking the place.

Sitting on Kale's cock, Sean convulsed, pumping the last of his orgasmic semen into the hair on Kale's chest, then sincerely said, "Gawd I wish this didn't have to be over. I'm not ready." He pensively stared down on Kale, or through him, like he was searching for his soul before he decided to disconnect from Kale lying face up beneath him.

"Wait. Don't move." Kale's eyes watered. Was he becoming soft? "Stay where you are, just like that. Please." His hands moved to Sean's chest, caressing every part of it, taking it in, and memorizing him. He blinked and a tear left the corner of his eye, flowing into the network of twisty flesh in his ear. "Dammit. I can't let you go. Not yet. Not like this."

Sean leaned forward and kissed Kale gently on the lips; transferring what might be love to the man he'd once clashed with. Suddenly his heart swelled for Kale; the man who opened his heart to him, opened his body, who he let penetrate him and cum in him. Sean held the kiss, and Kale did too.

Could love between them be blossoming in those few short days?

Kale wasn't strong anymore; the barrier that contained his emotions had crumbled. His heart ached and without Sean by his side, he didn't think he could survive. Another tear broke free, but this time he refused to let Sean see.

Chapter 19

Sean's flight was called prematurely. He shrugged and stuffed the pay-by-the minute cell phone into his satchel, it was all he had since his had been lost in the crash, and it was a piece of crap that would be trashed the minute he landed in L.A.

Kale and Sean said their goodbyes the night before and again that morning, keeping their emotions in-tact as best they could so the other wouldn't see how fragile they were.

Sean couldn't speak for Kale, but the last sex they had truly felt like the last, best, and most amazing fuck on earth. From screwing like raging addicts to making cool sweet love... It was perfect the way their rendezvous ended and for Sean it was never going to be that good with anybody. Never. He knew that, he could feel it. But there was always that hope for a next time, assuming they would have one.

When Sean made it to the boarding gate and lifted his ticket to be scanned, he stopped and plucked it back out of the attendant's hand, then hummed in a low voice only he could hear, "What am I doing? I can't do this without him. Dammit, I love him." His heart broke and his eyes went misty as he turned to face the way he had come.

Excusing himself to about fifty people standing in the boarding line, Sean pushed his way to the back of it, eager to escape.

Sean realized there was nothing more important than love, the love between two people who were drawn together, by force of nature or in a mysterious way. For him and Kale, it was clashingly mysterious. It started rough, but turned out right, and from what he could tell, could only get smoother.

Earlier Sean watched Kale walk away and that vision of him was not the one Sean wanted to carry as he moved on with life. It wasn't the way it was supposed to go. Something inside was prodding him, making him feel it. Was it his mind or his heart? Leaving was too painful and he would never manage without being able to see or know everything about Kale. He had to follow his heart, it was the only way. And with that he broke into a run, careening and colliding with people along the way.

At the passenger check-in point Sean had parted with Kale, only giving him a hug, and now he knew that wasn't enough. Why did he let the people around them stop that kiss he was aching to leave Kale with?

Sean figured Kale would no longer be where he left him, so he opted for making a dash to the car rental station instead. That made more sense.

He needed to get back to Kale before he packed up and left the bungalow for his hometown someplace on Kauai. That would be bad.

As Sean ran, more people got in his way, all seeming like they were purposely blocking him from getting that kiss from his pilot. He excused himself several times but nobody seemed to care. Shoulders knocked and a few heads turned. That was it, no sincere *I'm sorry* from anybody.

Sean made the corner into the main lobby where he collided with a muscular man, a handsome man, a man he could love. Breathless, Sean spoke, "You waited for me?" He blinked twice and then smiled. "What if I had gotten…?"

Kale interrupted Sean, moved closer, and took his hands; not caring if anybody saw him do it, didn't mind if the world knew he could love that man. "I had a feeling you weren't getting on that plane. The other part of your soul that lives in me said so." And then he kissed him.

Epilogue

Kale and Sean left the airport together. Sean smiled, thinking sweet thoughts of love.

Kale liked that part the best.

Sean and Kale considered making a home together. Kale grinned, thinking dirty thoughts of love.

Sean actually liked that part best.

THE
END

ABOUT THE AUTHOR

Gregory Jonathan Scott was born and raised in Grand Rapids, Michigan where he met Scott just out of high school and started a life with him before relocating to South Florida.

As a child, Gregory was always told he had a creative imagination and the artistic ability to transform a blank canvas into an eye catching work of art. Shortly after high school graduation, and together with his true love Scott, discovered the thrill of pottery and ceramic art. There was where the two of them opened a business for ceramists that rapidly became the first choice for any hobbyist, storefront and scholastic industry looking for supplies related to ceramics and pottery. During that time, Gregory was approached by art magazines to write short articles and educational columns pertaining to the ceramic artistry. Captivating readers by his writing style quickly grew, which ignited his desire to express himself further. Finding a love for writing, alongside his artistic hand, gave him inspiration to design and write M/M romance Novels.

Gregory and Scott are still together and are currently enjoying home life in South Florida with their lovable Shetland sheepdog and a sweet stray cat that showed up one day and decided to make their house her home.

OTHER WORKS BY
Gregory Jonathan Scott

TAKE TO THE SKY
THE PLANTATION AFFAIR
HEARTBREAK BEAT

Gregory Jonathan Scott